I0788532

The Fletcher's Gambit

Der Flechtemann Chronicle, Book 2

by G. L. Simon

Dedication

Sue, my wife, has been my constant companion and support for all our married life. In this second book she has been my constant alter ego listening to my reading of every chapter.

Thank you Sue for your love and encouragement in the pursuit of this endeavor for such a long time.

Acknowledgements

A word about dialect:

Using a foreign language is always difficult for a fiction writer, and, obviously, dialect is not a foreign language, but can appear so to the individual reader enjoying a good fiction. To that end, I have attempted to use a dialect for most of my characters in this and following books. The question can be asked, "is the dialect accurate? Well, let's just say I use a "salt and pepper" approach.

The dialect used for this book is based on middle English, though writing as such would render the passages to seem like a foreign language to most. So, I have taken the opportunity to mix a bit of middle English, tempered with a medieval flavor, in with modern English and use a reasonable Scottish brogue to do so. Too, one may ask why Scottish when the book is centered in Germany or then formally Saxony? That is a simple one, because a German dialect would necessitate writing in middle German which would make the story here untenable. I write, therefore, to give a flavor of an historic era of history for the enjoyment of my readership. Is the dialect totally accurate? No, but it is plausible.

Front cover graphic:

Openai.com rendering of the following request:

"Midieval mosaic in the hiberno-saxon style of a lichen covered warrior of the 14th century walking into a sunset his back to the viewer."

Thank You

Michelle, Lili, Jason, Luke and the rest of the project team at Book Writing Studios have been instrumental in the creation and publication of this book, Book 2, THE FLETCHER'S GAMBIT in the Der Flechtemann Chronicle series. Thank you

A Note from the Author

Now retired to my small acreage I find raising grapes and making wine provide me quite a bit of time to focus on writing a long thought-out series of books, a pursuit I wanted to do many years ago, but time was never available for such. Genealogy has always been an interest of mine but wanting to know more about my family 'Simon' name led me to want to follow the migration of the name and its iterations across the globe. In this mix, too, is the what-if thoughts of the name in other ages in history as it relates to the common person through the lens of history. Where had the name been? Why did or does it change? These questions and many more have led me to this place. Studying the etymology of the name is genealogy of a different nature.

Too, I am interested in the eons of the social life of humankind. I know technologies change and knowledge grows faster with each generation. It would seem we may implode someday for want of something to design or think about. However, my generational interest falls into the area of social and physical survival. That being said, it is my contention that a person today, 500 years ago, or 50,000 years ago are all driven by the same concerns: food, shelter, safety and social connectivity. My stories focus on those facets of life.

The stories to be pondered then may be "Did the people of yesteryear have encounters which deprived them of these different necessities?" The assumed answer being 'yes' leads us then to consider "Were these tasks or necessities pursued much as humans do today?" So, my stories encompass the 'yes' of the question by attempting to tell tales through the lense of history that show how this may well be true. Are all of the stories factual socially or historically, not really, but they are possibilities. Many of the historical events of my stories, however, did take place even

though a fiction writer is prone to bend events to meet their
characters' needs and the plot's arc.

Table of Contents

Prologue

"Father, I saw you today.

Today, the old pains returned…[only for] a moment, but I shook within. Such terrible chances does a man survive! And all the while looking, looking forever at the one certainty…the abyss before him.

[Yet] he spins his dice each day, and each gambit is peace for a moment…even if only for another sweet moment."

-Brother Jakob, circa 1384/1385

In the hushed solitude of the half-green church courtyard, a venerable old monk named Jakob sought refuge from the chill of the morning. A monk of advanced years, the old man's frail frame was sang the dirge of relentless years gone by too fast. He sat upon a crude stone bench, hunched and haggard, bathed in the feeble sunlight that seeped through the looming arches of the abbey's aged architecture.

through the looming arches of the abbey's aged architecture.

With his coarse black robes draped over bony shoulders, Jakob's mind flickered nowadays between present and past. Sometimes he would stop being the old priest altogether. Sometimes, when the apples would ripen here, he would be back on the road, or back at the farm…or back at the battlefields, back in the dark, cold forests, back on the marches that never stopped. A man of earthly battles and

1

worldly ambitions in his youth, now those martial days ended, he found a rebel dwelt within him. However, these secrets lay dormant now, concealed beneath his piety like ancient treasures buried deep within the earth.

Old Jakob, now a man of ailing eccentricities both in his demeanor and his speech, sometimes would stare off, looking at nothing in particular. Often he awakened from a deep sleep screaming. When he spoke, whether in local dialect or in latin, his voice possessed a peculiar cadence, as if the words he uttered danced on the precipice between profundity and madness. His voice, each syllable pronounced with a delicate quiver, raspy and trembling, akin to the rustling of autumn leaves,

Seated there, Jakob yearned to speak, to share the many musings that swirled within the labyrinthine corridors of his mind. Yet, his monastic vows and the weight of his faith shackled his tongue. He knew some secrets, like silent echoes in the vast nave of a cathedral, were meant to remain unrevealed—at least while he lived. The other monks of Nienburgh Abbey already regarded the old man with a mixture of bemusement and indifference. To them, he ghosted the halls a living paradox, an oddity best left undisturbed in the obscure corners of the cloister. They paid him little heed as they went about their daily devotions and rituals, content to let him linger in his solitude.

As Jakob basked in the meager warmth of the sun's embrace, his ancient eyes scanned the courtyard, tracing the intricate patterns of the aged cobblestones beneath his feet.

With a laborious sigh, he reached between the pages of the caliginous book on his lap, producing a weathered scrap of paper. The yellowed fragment from his past lay in the grasp of weathered fingers, a remnant of his youthful aspirations to possess the mysteries of Latin. Lines and

2

symbols adorned the parchment—marks of his desperate attempts to learn.

As Jakob studied the scrap, a bell rung and his gaze shifted toward the horizon, where the distant towers of the abbey loomed. A faint rustling of robes heralded the arrival of a young monk, nameless and faceless to Jakob's weakened memory and eyes, assigned to care for the elder brothers.

"Come hither, boy," Old Jakob said, voice atremble.

"Aye," the young monk said as he approached Jakob with a barely-perceptible sigh, his semi-dutiful presence familiar by now. As the boy reached Jakob's side, his hands deftly produced a small jar of ointment, a supposed remedy for the gout-swolen knees that often plagued the aged monk. With practiced care, the youth uncorked the jar, revealing an overly fragrant concoction of herbs and oils.

Jakob's eyes, weathered and world-weary, remained fixed on imaginary, distant horizon. The parchment lay forgotten on his lap, its latin codes whispering secrets long closed to any meaningful understanding. Before his old eyes, the courtyard, bathed in the soft glow of sunlight, yet again became a convergence of past and present, where memories mingled with the mundane. A hooded man with a bow and arrow appeared to stand at the fog edge of his murky vision. Jakob turned, and—

Jerked to awareness, no vision sat at the fringes of his sight – of course.

The boy, meanwhile continued the rudiments of his task, dipped his fingers into the ointment and began to rub it gently onto Jakob's leg, where age had etched lines of pain and weariness. As the boy worked, Jakob's mind wandered, retracing the fragments of his past.

In a voice that carried the weight of years, Jakob began to speak. He spoke not of grand battles or heroic exploits, but of half-forgotten dreams and the elusive allure of youth. His reminiscences now vague, as if the mists of time blurred the edges of his memories.

"I was once a—what was I?" he muttered, his voice akin to the hush of the breeze amongst ageless oaks. "A simple soul with a notion, aye-aye, I had such notions. I pursued 'em and crafted 'em, and otheres… they weaved their own schemes. I those times, ere I sought refuge in this holy sanctuary, I witnessed the machinations of men…"

The boy listened, his eyes fixed on his task, his ears worn out by the old man's words. Jakob's disjointed fragments of stories passed by the boy's ears before—many, many times. Jakob's cryptic tales hinted of a life once lived beyond the confines of the monastery. The lad once sought some deeper, more curious meaning to the meanders of Jakob's past. Curiosity, however, now found a memory shelf on which to set the ramblings and replace with complacent smiles.

As Jakob continued to mutter, his gaze fell back upon the scrap of paper, as if noticing the yellowed notes for the first time. He picked the parchment up again with trembling fingers--the symbols now half-faded.

"Ah, the gentle tongue of Latin," Jakob pondered, now conversing in this foreign speech, his gaze once more lost in thought. "My initial lessons… they came from a venerable comrade. Or perhaps companion—or was he a companion? Adversary? I cannot say."

The boy continued his ministrations, and in the tranquil courtyard, the boundaries between past and present continued to blur. The weight of history settled upon Jakob's old shoulders like the tired mantle of time.

"You see, lad," Jakob started, his voice a hoarse whisper, "We lead our lives, we all do… yet that which has gone is never truly gone. All that departs returns, first as recollection, and then as envy."

The boy nodded, unhearing, his eyes never leaving his task; however, a smirk of a smile curled at the edges of his lips. This time though the courtyard seemed to hold its breath, as if anticipating new revelations that lingered on the old monk's tongue.

Jakob's gaze remained fixed on the parchment in his hand, his fingers tracing the lines of forgotten Latin characters as he muttered. "Such plans, such notions…"

The boy's curiosity stirred, drawn to a change in the old monk's voice. Still, however, young monk maintained his silent vigil. He knew better than to expect much sense from the Jakob. In any case, four more elderly monks needed to receive his attention on this morning.

"There was a season," Jakob murmured, his eye twitching beneath the burden of concealed verities, "when I possessed naught. Now, I own naught-yet-all. So similar, and yet not quite so… then as envy."

The boy's brow furrowed slightly, a flicker of concern in his otherwise composed countenance. The old man sounded more mad than usual today. He wondered if he should call someone.

In that very instant, Jakob glanced upward, as if from slumbering thought. "My knees are shining quite sufficient," he chuckled. "Go tend to the other aged bones akin to mine.

5

Fare well, lad, fare thee well…" Pointing to the door Jakob whispered, "In God's name, boy, go!"

Shaking his head, the young monk took his leave.

Now alone, Jakob opened the book at his lap to place the old page back. Remembering the difficulty writing once presented to him, his hands unthinkly traced his own aberrant, rambling etchings,

"Ah my Father, such gifts you gave me," the old man said sadly. "And such joys you took away."

With weariness he retrieved ink and stylus from their hiding place behind a loose stone in his cloister. For months the hiding place served as a secret enclave for his reminiscing. He carefully selected a new sheet of parchment from the opus which accompanied the ink and writing tip. Anchoring the new leaf on his small table he slowly began to write, blinking to stay awake in the chill.

"Father," he muttered as he wrote. "I saw…you today…"

Chapter I: Seeker's Luck

-Brother Jakob, circa 1382

As the shine of the evening sun slowly faded, his eyes teared from hours of reading and the last rays of the day, Michael Simon leaned back in his chair. He rubbed the dampness from the corners of his eyes as he examined once again the *magnum opus* on the table before him. A welling grin of satisfying excitement grew from deep within and edged itself to the corners of his mouth reflecting on the unbelievable discovery of journal pages written in the hand of Jakob the Monk.

"*...Each gambit is peace for a moment,*" Michael repeated the text slowly, shaking his head at the profound statement.

Michael Simon, seated in his corner booth, savored the ambiance of the diner in which he sat, a modest establishment, exuded a nostalgic charm, with an unpretentious facade. The interior of the diner, spotlessly clean, bore the marks of decades of important passing found in time. The linoleum floors to the rows of laminate-topped tables and vinyl-upholstered chairs spoke of contemporary good times and far-reaching medieval happenings. The structure, a place where memories were made, stories told, and the echoes of the past lingered in every creaking floorboard and well-carved under-table. The walls, adorned with faded photographs and vintage posters from a bygone era, affectively heightened the ambiance of the smiles and laughter passed from customer to customer. In this unpretentious haven, Michael found a moment of respite and a chance to reflect on the legacy of his own enigmatic ancestor.

The patrons, mostly locals, sat in quiet camaraderie, their conversations punctuated by the occasional burst of laughter. Regulars occupied their usual spots, engaged in animated discussions over cups of strong coffee or mugs of frothy beer.

In his contemplative solitude, he mused over the possibility, being a relative and all, he might bear a resemblance to this old cleric. Though there were no known portraits of Jakob the Monk, and understanding heredity, Michael assumed, certain traits passed on to succeeding generations. Of course, Michael sighed, he was much younger—or at least seemed apparent, than his distant family member. In his sixty-odd years on this earth, Michael exercised regularly and stayed in quite good shape. Even now, at his age he could pass for a man of just fifty or so years. His tall frame and gracefully gray hair continued to give him stature among his peers and their wives. But his eyes told the truth—they were the eyes of an older man, a man who continued to grieve and understand great loss. Now a year and a bit since his wife died of cancer, Michael still felt the tug of grief, the loss of a soulmate.

As Michael traced the faded ink with his weathered fingers, he could not help but wonder about the old monk's words. *Each gambit is peace for a moment.* Michael thought he understood the term, but shadows of the unknown crept into his total understanding. *Any gambit attempted to move ahead in this unveiling of his puzzle did give 'peace for a moment'* Michael supposed. Of course, for him, finding of this journal produced exciting information. The ancient book, a relic from a distant past, marked the first hint he found of his family—the Simon family.

Michael's son Gary and daughter-in-law, Vivian, filled a void from which he thought he would never recover. The emptiness without Rachel brought about a terrible depression to fight through. Agonizing days of loneliness stretched into months, but with Gary's strength and Vivians's gentleness, Michael remembered the promise of *"go forth"* made to Rachel. His wife, once a part of the quest he now found himself pursuing, remembrances of discussions now emerged through the day to day attempts to sort a future. The two planned excursions and saved pennies for quite some time to pursue the family name. Now, Michael's heart broke for the old man, whose thoughts, and ideas of a yesteryear scribbled on the parchments of this ancient book, sat in a cloistered abbey with no one to understand him.

His thoughts drifted to Yakov, by the solitary journey of a life devoted once to family, then to cause, and finally to faith. He could not help but wonder how Yakov—or Jakob—felt then, without family by his side at the end of life with his secrets and regrets kept locked within the confines of the monastery.

Hesitating for a moment, Michael reached for his phone, a lifeline to the world outside this nostalgic reverie. He dialed a familiar number, and after a few rings, a voice on the other end answered.

"Hello?"

"Gary," Michael said, smiling slightly. "It's your old man. How are you doing, son?"

Gary's response was immediately warm and affectionate. "Hey, Dad! Sorry, didn't notice the number. I'm doing great. Just finished my shift—I'm taking Vivian over to that Thai place she likes. Everything's going smoothly here. How about you, globetrotter?"

Michael, holding back a chuckle, his heart swelling for a moment, listening to his son's familiar voice. "Just sitting in a diner, taking time to think."

A pause echoed on the other end of the line. Michael imagined his son furrowing his brow in concern. "So, everything okay, Dad? You sound a bit...contemplative."

Michael nodded, a quiet acknowledgement, "Yeah, son, everything's fine. I was just thinking about…" he paused, not knowing how to respond with specifics, then quickly continued. "…well, the works. Got a lot of digging around to do."

"And you're the man to do it," Gary said with confidence but equally as vague. Michael could hear traffic behind Gary and knew he must be in downtown somewhere.

"Well, I best get back to it," Michael said awkwardly, but feeling somewhat better. "I've forgotten why I called."

They both laughed.

"It's alright dad," there was a a pause. "You know you can just call, right? You don't need a reason."

"Sure," Michael smiled. Just then, looking up at a movement across the room from him, the diner's door opened to reveal a familiar, bespectacled figure. James

Walsh, as red-headed and eager as ever. Michael waved at him from his corner. "Son, I've got to go. James is here."

"The guy helping you?"

"Yes, my partner in time," Michael joked. Gary groaned on the other end.

"That was terrible, dad." Gary said with a smirk.

"I know," Michael chuckled. "Talk t'you later, son."

"Bye, dad."

Michael tapped the call-cancel icon on his cell phone just as James arrived with two large shredded coconut with chocolate chip cookies on a plate.

"The *Guten Tisch* serves complementary cookies every morning," James explained while Michael looked at him skeptically.

"How did you not know that?" Michael asked. "Ah, the advantage of being 'hiesig,'" He nodded smiling, inching the book away. "Don't get any crumbs on this."

"Aha, very good, you are getting the hang of the language, pretty soon you vill be 'local' too. However, relax," James said, holding his hands up in mock surrender. "I'd shoot myself if I got crumbs all over the greatest historical discovery of our lifetimes."

"You think this is that important?"

"Better, my friend—I know it," said James, pointing at the book in a soft confident voice. "Dis find is very valuable."

"I agree with you then," Michael said. "James, I've been making progress with the later Latin passages in

Jakob's journal—you know, the ones written in a strange code? It's like he forgets what language he's writing in. The job to do so is tough, but the more I get into this journal, the more I grasp how deep his thoughts go. Age took its toll, but his memories are so...*vivid.* Sometimes I feel as if I am reading literature from the nineteenth century.

James nodded, his gaze shifting between the journal and Michael. "I've been concentrating on the Old German sections," he replied, his tone reflective. "It's fascinating to see how language has changed over the centuries. Jakob's words offer a glimpse into a world that's long past."

Michael couldn't agree more. "It's like peeling back the layers of time. Each word he wrote is a thread connecting me to family history."

James picked up a menu and idly flipped it open. "You know, Michael, I've been pondering about something. Jakob vas an odd man, as we've learned from zis journal. He vas unclear about his knowledge of Latin, and I can't help but vunder if there's more to dat tale."

Michael's interest was piqued. "What do you mean?"

James leaned in, lowering his voice. "How did he learn it? Who taught it to him? I can't imagine der Flechtemann knew it either. He was, after all, just a conventional fletcher before he started fightin'."

Their conversation was interrupted by the arrival of a waitress, who took their orders for coffee. Once she left, Michael eyed James, who was already done with his cookie.

"No coffee spills," he said, and James chuckled. "But you're right, James. It'll be fascinating to see how he achieved his education for us to know more about him. We owe it to him, the world, and, well,..." Michael released a long audible breath, "… to our own curiosity to get deeper into this."

"Ya, ya," James said, grinning.

"I noticed you brought your bagpack along," Michael commented. Sure enough, James shouldered his worn-out knapsack.

"Full of reference and personal notes," James said. "I could just have brought everything over on my cellphone but…well you know me, I still like to have hard paper copies and physical written notes, ja."

Michael chuckled. "Good to know I'm not the only living fossil around here. So, we're getting back into it then?"

"Ja, I'm all set whenever you are."

***

"It's funny how things work," Michael mused.

They were back at his hotel room with their notes strewn over a round wooden desk. The dark red grain of its surface gleamed under the warm electronic lighting as translucent sheets of notes spread there like allotments of land. At the center of this almost topographical setup, the ancient tome sat open like a great church, central to life in this ecosystem of ancient knowledge.

"Hm?" James said, distracted. He scanned through his notepad scribbling with the ardor of an obsessed academic—exactly his demeanor.

Michael knew this research was a major breakthrough for James, and with an academic background of his own, Michael also knew the rarity of actually getting to do such work.

"Was just saying, it's funny how stuff works," Michael acknowledged. "It's like what Yakov surmised—we've been taking chances all along to get here. And now, we've hit a treasure trove of information."

"We'll need a bit more, though," James said, squinting. "Old Jakob here has all the chronological continuity of an absurdist drama—he's switched between three different time periods just on this page, ja."

"Age catches up with you," Michael said somberly. The muddling of the mind, the passage of years, brought personally unknown fears to him. He knew exactly how Jakob might confuse time. For he knew more than a few older friends who displayed disorientation with age.

"You're right," James said, sounding a bit frustrated. But it's also confusing to read. Feels like I'm reading *Ulysses*—in a completely different language, ja!"

"The Latin codes were serious stuff," Michael said, lips pressed tight. "They seemed pretty basic when I dug into them. I found out they originated from ancient Roman codes in Caesar's time. It's not that strange, really, since they were in use up until the 16th century. But no one on any forum has ever come across these codes used in any correspondence outside of Rome."

"Very curious here. Exactly my meaning." James scratched the back of his head, a qwerk he often exhibited when confused. Then pointing at a page of the journal, he continued. "How did Jakob know these things? It doesn't make sense."

"Well," Michael said, leaning forward to squint at the book between them. "Only one way to find out."

Chapter II: The Valley

"In each tale I find, the valley preceeds the bright mountain. The low preceeds the high; the belly [of the beast] preceeds salvation. Such is the Lord's writ, thinks I: to know light is to arrive through the dark..."

-Brother Jakob, circa 1383

Yakov Symon yawned awake.

A blessedly dreamless night—a rarity, Yakov, propping himself on one elbow, looked around, scratching his growing stubble. Next to him, his brother Dieter still slept, his wide shoulders covered by a ratty cloak, his long dark hair covering his eyes. His sister, Anna, taken to waking far earlier than any of them, to give her more time to prepare for meals of the day, left a noticeably empty spot in the tent. Yawning again, Yakov threw back the furs covering him and stood as best he could in the crampt space. He belted his tunic and stooped further in his effort to exit the threadbare tent, carrying a tattered black chaperon grabbed from where it lay under his head's resting place. Throwing his hood over his head so it offered some warmth to his ears. He curled its long tail around his neck for extra comfort then stepping into the day's light, took time to look over the camp.

The undisciplined retinue Yakov first met after his capture in the melee with der Flechtemann sometime past now spread its well-organized camp amidst a patch of sprawling wilderness. Reunited now with his leader father, Hans Symon, his sister Anna and brother Deiter, Yakov did not assume the nature of his captors to be that of an unorganized rabble.

The men were dirty-faced and bearded. The women cleaned stoves in the water of a drying creek, and the cold sun did not warm the scarred sentries as they stood lookout in an octagonal formation around the camp. Those sentries wore cloaks draped with shaggy tufts of moor-grass to make them nearly invisible from a distance. Their hard eyes surveyed the horizon. One of them nodded at Yakov as he passed.

Now quite aware the resistance fighters did not present a disarray of wondering peasants. He knew they formed an onerous army to disrupt the commerce and trade of wealthy merchants, merciless landowners, and corrupt clergy who placed the burden of their indulgences on the backs of the common people. Even though on a strained footing with his father, Hans, der Flechtemann, he found some sympathy with this band of orphaned friends.

Hidden amongst the foliage and resting in what once may have been a small forest, half-cleared by some passing loggers for wood, lay the camp itself. Concealed here the haphazard collection of makeshift tents and lean-tos created a rough affair for the resistance fighters. Cautious urgency encouraged the need to protect themselves from Petres the Chain, the relentless mercenary hired by the Archbishop, who now pursued them with the fervor of a pack of wolves. The Chain and his men doggedly chased the organization of partisans across the Empire throughout the short summer. Der Flechtemann, forced in a desperate bid to shake his pursuers, led his band south.

17

Der Flechtemann's plan—and Yakov was sure one existed—still seemed opaque. Now a recognized member of the congregation of patriots, Yakov, and Anna's special friend Sieghart, both gone from camp for a fortnight on sortie and returning the previous evening, stood in the morning light and acknowledged those around as he looked for a man named Nerijus, a cheerful Baltic man. Important information needed to be passed to him for further movement of the rebels towards the Alps, letting the treacherous terrain obscure their tracks.

In mid-autumn the weather turned brutally to a biting chill. The once-vibrant leaves of the forest surrendered to the cold, their bright hues of green replaced by reds and browns. Each morning brought with it a thin dusting of almost-snow that clung to the world like a shroud, causing the rebels to huddle closer to the flickering warmth of their campfires. At their posts, the sentries rubbed their hands absently.

Nerijus sitting staring into the light of an early morning campfire looked up as Yakov approached. Squating near by he relayed information gathered for the trek ahead and details of pitfalls along the way. Yakov and Seigert saw no great problems with the move other than urgency and the time of the year—winter near the mountains brought its own problems for survival. Nerijus would lead the group to higher ground in the mountains as soon as camp was struck in the mid morning.

Yakov, finding a place to relieve himself, made his way back to the fire. He looked at the sihlouettes of the mountains in the distance. Yakov could see the possibility of shelter and sanctuary there, but he also knew the snow and bitter cold awaited them in the higher altitudes. The path to those mountains clear for now, would close soon. He could not help but wonder if der Flechtemann's audacious gamble would pay off. The Alps were unforgiving by all accounts, and a frozen death did not appeal to him.

Moving past some rebels pulling down the tents, Yakov sat on a dead log near their campfire, his gaze fixing upon his sister Anna as she stirred a bubbling pot of soup. The fire crackled like the determination that always seemed to burn within her. Her hands reacted deftly as she added a pinch of dried herbs and a meagre handful of vegetables to the pot, her movements guided by a quiet expertise. Her blonde hair tied back in a makeshift bun, with smudges of soot and dirt adorning her fair cheeks, in all this though the deep understanding green eyes Yakov knew all to well, those eyes of care and understanding, shined through.

"Guten Morgen," she said without turning, tasting the soup with a finger. She made a face and added another pinch of herbs.

"Morgen t'ye, sister," Yakov replied. After a moment of silence, he cleared his throat. "The soup smells well."

"Ye have it twice a day, Yakov," Anna rolled her eyes. "The smell rises as it always does."

"Truth," Yakov smiled, then looked around. "Is he…?"

"He's not here yet," Anna said shortly.

Shaken to the core by the revealed identity of der Flechtemann as their father opened wounds from his long absence. None were more affected by this than Anna whose anger ran deep and would be slow to heal. Anna found it difficult to engage in conversation about him without a tinge of bitterness.

Yakov sensed her discomfort regarding their father and changed the subject. "Dieter does live well to camp life, rightly better than I. He's grown into a strong-limbed boy— he'll be as hale as a hardy Hillman in another year, I'd reckon."

Anna's expression softened as she chuckled. "Hale and wise as an old man, our Dieter. But he's young yet."

"Come, sister, he's a man in his own right by now— although I admit I was a rightly fool at his age," Yakov smiled. "But then, I've always had a fool livin' within me. Have thee remembrance of that time I tried to cajole a rabbit into the farmstead? Remember the commotion it caused?"

Anna chuckled, her infectious laughter like a fleeting melody in the night. "Oh, goodness! How could one forget Old Karl in a right tizzy? Ye reckoned ye'd brought us a grand feast, but it turned into a wild run through the stubble strewn fields, with me trailing close behind ye with a very long stick.

Yakov returned the momentary amusement, the memory bringing a sense of nostalgia. "'Twas quite a sight, seeing ye chase a rabbit tearin' through the grasses. And, it got away in the end, aye it did?"

Anna nodded with a smile. "Aye, it did. Ye were rightly disappointed—but come the morrow, it gave us all a good laugh though, 'cept for that brined old sot of an uncle Karl. They were handsome days." She paused reflecting melancholy. "Sometimes I wish we could return there."

"Aye, 'twas they were," Yakov agreed. "Simpler, too. Now, I… I know ken what to think." Leaning forward, he asked in a whisper, "Anna, does ye…art thou still convinced in Father's cause? About this uprising o' his, I mean."

20

Anna's stirring paused for a moment, and she looked up at him, her gaze steady. "You mean *der Flechtemann?*"

"Aye," Yakov nodded, his uncertainty etched on his face. "Yea, him. He's brought us to the base of those mountains," he said tilting his head to the snow-covered peaks beyond. "...and why Petris the Chain's hounds fear his crop more than our arrows. I ain't rightly sure, sister."

Anna's expression grew solemn as she continued to stir the soup with thoughtful determination. "I know thou hath doubts, Yakov. But the Lord knows what He knows, and He hath brought ye and I to fa... to this cause." Again, she paused, lifting her ladle from the soup she pointed it in Yakov's direction. "That man, our own Hans Symon, yea our Father, has a dream."

She relaxed and began stirring the soup once more, continuing with renewed affirmation, she pledged, "I ken him not, but I follow the dream still. Them crown heads and tonsured robber-barons stamp down at the common folk, and aye, I'd make even me own truce with *the devil* t'do some reasonable good in this world."

Her eyes flashed as she finished. Expressionless, Yakov reflected as he studied the pot while it simmered with Anna's caring attention, the scent of the cooking soup filling the air. "Believe it so Anna, I willingly desire to believe; yet, we've been on the run for so long. It feels as if we're one fall from bein' caught with our small britches down, prepared fer a swift spear in our bare behinds lookin' in the wrong direction."

"Quiet now, yer talkin' like a gruff warrior," Anna scolded as she set down her stirring spoon and turned towards him. "Listen here, we've journeyed this far, my dear Yakov. We've faced many a hardship and confronted real peril side by side. Should I surrender now? Oh, aye, that man's full of faults, but still, it's the dream we're striving for."

Yakov let out a long sigh, his uncertainty still nagging at him somewhere in the back of his mind trust was difficult. "I ken your meanin' sister. It's just... a-times, I worry fer us."

Anna reached out, placed a firm but gentle hand on his strong shoulder to give determination to her promise. Her touch comforting, she reassured Yakov, "That ye worry is yer virtue. But mine mind is made."

Yakov sighed, and gave her a smile. "Then mine is as well."

Just then, from beyond the camp's perimeter, the faint shudder of hooves hitting grass could be heard. The sentries stiffened, their senses alert, now other rebels stood, some with arrows nocked, prepared for what may come. Yakov and Anna exchanged a quick knowing glance.

As the sound drew nearer, a small group of riders emerged from the shadows, their horses snorting, steam rising from their flanks in the chilly air. The assumed leader rode at the forefront, his hood pulled low over his head, obscuring most of his features except for his shaggy grey beard and a nose, ruddy from the cold. Once known simply as Hans Symon, now der Flechtemann, the infamous rebel, subject of stories throughout the Empire. Behind him, his scouts followed in single file. Some were hooded like him, while others let their hoods fall back, revealing faces marked by exhaustion and dirt. A ragtag bunch dressed in worn tunics and cloaks bore the signs of countless nights spent charting the Chain's relentless pursuit.

Der Flechtemann, reined in the strong andalusian as his scouts followed suit. With a quiet grace he dismounted, his bow and arrow slung over his shoulder. He approached the campfire where Yakov and Anna stood waiting.

No need for unintended words, Yakov's eyes met his father's, a silent understanding passing between them. The scouts return brought news—news that could shape the fate of the young rebellion.

Der Flechtemann, after a pause, waiting for welcome wishes to settle down, spoke, recognizing the question in his band's eyes, his voice distinctively low and gravely. "Aye mates, we've seen signs of the Chain's lads closin' in. The dogs, they be not far away."

Anna looked at him questioning with determination in her eyes. "What's our next move?"

Der Flechtemann's gaze flickered as if hesitant to meet Anna's eyes. He diverted his attention toward the white peaks of the distant mountains. Listen up, all of ye!" Returning his attention to the gathered band before him, he bellowed for everyone in the camp to hear. "In two nights' time, we'll make for a secret vale we've spied. A safe haven to rest our bones and plan ahead—Sieghart's already there, with two men, makin' way. But we can't dally if we aim to march south 'cross these peaks. Winter's frost be gnawin', and the cursed Chain's grip be tightenin' every day."

"Ho, der Flechtemann!" called Nerijus, emerging bleary-eyed from one of the tents. Left temporarily incharge, Nerijus was not a tall man, through strong-armed and quick-eyed. His thinning brown hair and high cheekbones gave him a strangely graceful appearance to Yakov's eye.

"Well-met," der Flechtemann replied, raising an eyebrow. "Things must go well here, if ye hath the luxury of such long rest."

23

Nerijus scratched at his beard looked appropriately chastised. "'Pologies fer mine tardiness. But things, betwixt ye and I, do not fare well at all, neither in journey, nor in camp. In our passin' to this place we encountered deserted homesteads, and twice, came across men who had hung themselves, their noses and lips blister'd o'er. Some blight has appeared in these regions."

"I, too, have seen the signs," der Flechtemann said quietly. "And what of our camp? Any afflicted?"

"Nay, though we are afflicted by a…*different* blight," Nerijus said, glancing at Yakov as he sat nearby. "Well, you tell 'im, lad."

Yakov nodded, looking at his father. "Morale wanes. We follow yer command, marchin' southward. Already, we see the mountains on the horizon, when the sky be clear and rain does not soak our heads. But doubt breeds doubt, and we fear what we find in them mountains—I hear folk fear of freezin' while passin' o'er."

Der Flechtemann sighed, irritation in his voice. "Why do they worry so? Have I ever led them astray, Nerijus? Ye answer me."

"Nay," Nerijus squirmed. "But-"

"*But,*" Anna interjected, looking coolly at the rebel leader. "'Tis thine fault, not theirs. Ye spoke a command like a prince, but explained it not to yer supposed brothers. Is that not contrary to the beliefs of ye? To the cause ye espouse?"

Der Flechtemann stiffened for an ungarded moment, then looked away to regain self-control. Breathing slowly he regarded the band once more. "Ye speak true. Men!" he called out loudly. "Men! Women, children, all ye folk, lend me but a moment!"

24

A curious bustle rippled through the band as the rebels trickled towards the fireplace. With surprising litheness for his age, the rebel leader leapt atop a nearby log. Standing tall beside Yakov, der Flechtemann waited for a moment, his hands on his waist as the rebels gathered around. From their tent, a bleary-eyed Dieter emerged, rubbing his sore neck as he leaned against a tree, watching the rebels beginning to trickle towards the fire.

Dieter shot Yakov a glance, as if to ask, What's afoot?

Yakov simply shrugged.

"E'er since I returned from my fruitless hunt for that dog Petres," he began in a loud, gravely voice, "I have decided that we shall move south. Such is yet trust in me, that ye have complied, come doubt, come sweat, come toil. Ye have worn out yer soles in respect, and I respect such trust in turn—fer I am no prince, only a brother amongst a brotherhood."

At this Anna shot him a look, but remained silent.

"But o'course," he continued, looking from face to face. "Ye have had yer questions, have wondered why we flee the flame behind us unto the clutches of the frost on yon peaks and passes. Ye wonder and clutch yer children close, and think the old bastard hath perhaps finally lost 'is mind."

A nervous chuckle ran through those assembled. Some of the rebels looked ashamed. Yakov wondered at this change. Faces that only a few days ago, darkened with doubt and distrust, suddenly seemed reassured and bright, a sort of light restored within some distant reach of them.

"But the truth be that mine intention is not fer us t'hide among those treacherous stony places there," der

Flechtemann said, pointing vaguely towards the distant mountains. "And…" He paused, "there is no purpose in fleeing into Italia, fer the arm o'the church rests even heavier in that land of fat lords and corrupt bishops. Nay, mine plan is a mite more devious. We shall lure that poxed bastard up behind us as we climb, and lose him in the winding passes. Let 'im think we flee this Empire. Let 'im think, even, we are in some cave, licking brine from a stony fang. Let 'im freeze his buttocks off, chasing shadows in the snow!" der Flechtemann roared, a glint in his eye.

A round of unapologetic laughter and loud applause erupted from the partisan band. As Yakov watched, he caught a quick glimmer of respect in Anna's eye, then suddenly scowling, fearful of being caught in an unarmed moment, she returned to stirring the soup.

"Now, the bastards behind us gain each moment we waste, so drive sleep from thine peepers and prepare! Break camp quickly, and we shall resume our deceptive march!" he commanded, iron in his voice.

The rebels understood the urgency of the situation immediately, and the camp stirred to life with a chorus of "aye's" and "hear hear's". Behind him, der Flechtemann's scouts, already dismounted, joined their comrades.

"What of the meal?" Anna asked coldly, speaking without looking at her father, as if the words were directed at the wind. "The wild onion is yet raw, but the broth is flavored enough, though watery."

"Aye, food will give us strength for our trek ahead," der Flechtemann replied, his voice neutral not wanting to emotionally give in to distraction with Anna. "But we shall take repast as we walk. Our foe Petris be close…we move now. Have we enough bowls?"

26

"Plenty."

"Well, that is sorted then," der Flechtemann nodded, his jaw tight as he walked past Anna. She continued to look forward with the same stony expression.

Yakov looked at her and hesitated.

"Are ye well?"

"Well as I may be," she said with bitter intent. "Come, help me move the stew. Ye can pass it out t'the folk fer me a-while. I needs wake our sleeping brother, lest they wrap his hibernating hide away with the tent."

"I'll help ye as well," Nerijus said morosely. "best get used t'handing out soup—he's never trustin' me in command ever again. Curse my drowsy hide!"

***

Early dawn crept into the sky as the siblings dragged themselves along in the rear of the rebel march, bone-tired and sneezing, along a gentle downward slope. Venturing deeper into the valley, the sky lightened and birdcalls broke the silence of their shuffling gate. The wooded beauty unfolded in all its grandeur as the land beneath their feet undulated gracefully, revealing ancient meadows. Strange, carved waystones lay fallen on overgrown trails. Yakov wondered at the folk who lived in such places in the early eons of the world.

The group of displaced partisans passed dense copses filled with crackling oaks and gnarled pines, shuffling beside sheer cliffs whose daunting height scraped the heavens. The thick tangled foliage, as an added boon aided to conceal the group's presence, allowing to at least slow the Chain's forces as well.

Winding streams meandered through the landscape. Waterways carved winding paths through the dark valley, cutting the land deeper through ages of erosion. Alongside the other trekkers, Yakov, Anna, and Dieter dipped their hands into the icy water, drinking in the cool draught.

"'Tis true-cold," Anna shivered, rubbing numb fingers. "I'd wash mine face, if it were only a mite warmer."

They could not stay long in one place, however.

As Yakov walked alongside Anna and Dieter in this serene valley, he couldn not help but compare it with the chaos of battle and the twisted ideals of the Holy Roman Church. The valley, dark and threatening as it appeared, seemed to be a world apart from the horrors of the battlefield. Here, the only sounds were the calls of birds and the gentle murmur of water. The only battle waged came against the biting chill in the frigid air.

Anna broke the whisper of silence, sensing his searching thoughts. "Ye've come a long way from yer gruesome days in the Abbot's service Yakov."

He guffawed without humor. "Yet them days chafe at our heels as we speak. Somewhere back there, the old beast still chases me." Yakov retorted.

His arms crossed, Dieter chimed in, "Yer past may haunt ye, but 'tis not only thou that is pursued. We fly from the same peril, together—better than being haunted alone."

Anna nodded in agreement, smiling comfortingly at Yakov. "Our little brother speaks well. We travel now together—and 'tis what matters."

Yakov considered their wise words, the weight of his past and the uncertainty of his future pressing upon him. "Aye, yer right. I have little cause t'complain."

A birdcall nearby sounded immediately strange to Yakov. In a moment, the marching column halted. At the head of the rebels, der Flechtemann paused and matched the call.

From behind a shadow of trees, Sieghart and another man appeared to meet der Flechtemann. After they talked, the two men made their way down the column, clapping the backs of the others as they passed. Yakov noted now grown longer if not thicker, Sieg's once slight beard created a swirling wild appearance to the young friend of Anna's authority. A fortnight ago Yakov last saw der Flechtemann's intrepid second-in-command. His blond curls, tied back, he grinned as Anna blushed to see him. The man next to Sieg looked dour by comparison, with his deeply pockmarked face and somber eyes. He seemed strangely familiar to Yakov.

The moment his searching eyes caught Yakov's, the man's expression changed. Immediately alert, his hand fell to the long-knife on his belt as he hissed, "Who art thou?"

"Peace, Elias!" Sieg exclaimed, astonished. "Here is Yakov, brother to my Anna—though she is not yet mine," he hastily added, his confusion mounting on multiple levels.

Yakov squinted at the man. "I know thee from someplace."

"And I know thee," Elias said. "I never forget a visage, and I have seen thine attached to a soldier's mail in Schoningen."

"I've been there, aye," Yakov responded quietly, "and I remember you there not, but no surprise—many a face did I see, aye, many tears, many cries. Were I t'count…but nay, I do not count."

"What is this?" Elias said, looking at Sieg, incredulous. "Are we welcoming deserters now with open arms?"

"He's no deserter," Anna spat, moving between the two, her eyes ablaze. "he is brother t'me, and son to the man ye follow, so *hold yer tongue*."

Elias looked at them without expression for a moment, his eyes flitting from Yakov's ashen face, to Anna's fury, to cross-armed Dieter, looking at him with a furrowed brow. Finally, inclined his head. "Forgive me. Trust comes difficult to a man in these times."

"I understand yer meanin'," Yakov said quietly. Turning to his thoughts he wondered, *If this Elias was at Schoeningen, he was witness to the way the garrison acted.* Suddenly, Elias's reaction made more sense. A seed of self loathing now quivered through Yakov's memory of the events of that day.

"Why has the line halted?" der Flechtemann called from the front, looking back with a frown. "Is something awry?"

"Nay," Sieghart quickly yelled back. "All is well!" he then looked back between Yakov and Elias, as if to check whether all was, in fact, well.

"Aye," Elias said in a quiet voice eyeing Yakov more intently. "Yakov, I am sure I will remember more of ye in time—and perhaps, then, I shall trust thee. But mine trust is not easily won—so for the moment, forgive me this."

"As I said, I understand ye well," Yakov said soberly.

Nodding at them, Elias turned to Sieg. "I shall go see if my horse be well-fed. She can be temperamental."

Clapping Sieghart's shoulder, the pockmarked rebel moved further down the line. With him gone, Anna's attitude softened, and she smiled at Sieg as they began to move back a ways—markedly farther from himself and Dieter, Yakov noticed.

"Right disrespectful," Dieter muttered, and Yakov chuckled, looking at him.

"Ye say so for ye hasn't known love," Yakov admonished.

"And ye have?" Dieter asked with a raised eyebrow.

"Fairly scored," Yakov admitted, and left the sibling exchange at that.

In fact, truth be told, there was one girl, a times time ago, but just for a week between marches, he thought. He could still imagine the red-haired ghost of a thing with sunken cheeks and large eyes that could see into one's soul. How strange to think of her now, and how peculiar he felt, this sudden yearning for affection.

He walked on alone in quiet thought, yet not alone. *Of course, there was no time, never enough time,* Yakov thought, griping to himself. *Meeting over a bridge in her village for an hour or two in a day, with her speaking in a local dialect so thick...I never knew exactly what she was saying*. They kissed but once, and he noticed her blush as she ran off afterwards. The next day, he and his fellow men-at-arms were back at march. As the regiment passed over Yakov remembered surveying the bridge and yearning for one last look at his new found love. In the midday sun, however, without the wave of a friend to send him off, the structure stood desolate, an unwelcome reminder of his station at a time in the past while in the employ of the Archbishop of Schoningen and his knights Niklas the Quick and Longbeard of Hesse.

Her name… uncertainty interrupted, and he felt his palms sweat. *I should be able to remember her name.* He chided. *It was…Odilia. Or was it? No, it must have been Odilia. I would not forget.* He reassured himself.

With this decided, Yakov blinked away his memories. The column of partisans now walked uphill. Beside him, Dieter looked intently at the trees as if trying to burn their image into his mind. Just then, they found themselves passing into the clearing prepared for their arrival by Sieghart and Elias. Raised on a gentle, wooded cusp of land, the clearing found good protection on one side by heavy, creaking trees, and on the other by a sheer drop to a running stream. Four or five meters below the water sparkled in the sunlight. Yakov and Dieter, curious, took a cautious step forward to peek over the precipice.

"What say ye? Aye, I donna' think we could'a dune much better 'an this fer a gud winterin' camp?" Sieg said, striding with confidence into the middle of the broad grassy clearing, his arms spread wide and a Cheshire grin on his bearded face. "Well defended by the cliff o're their, well wooded for simple protection, and canna' be flanked from any approach. Elias and I, we already tore the most quarrelsome of the bushes dune, and as autumn did the rest of our chore, we dragged as many fallen branches away as possible, Aye, and—look there," he pointed, "behind that great rock!" Branches and sticks were neatly bundled already piled as fagots for fire. "And now, we have ourselves good, dry kindling as well. There is another path leadin' here, from below—or was," he chuckled with pride, "until we rolled a boulder down to block the ascent. We're safe and sound as can be."

"Well done, lads," der Flechtemann said to Sieg and Elias. Then looking at the rebels milling willy-nilly about around him, he roared, "By the heavens, do more than *gawk*, y'lot—set camp! We needs sleep t'confound the devil and ye will have much ado on the morrow."

Chapter III: The Curse

"Blessings and curses drive this pale earth —and the blessed, too, carry their own curses."

-Brother Jakob, circa 1382

On the next days dawn, Yakov awoke sweating, unable to breathe, the stench unbearable. The early morning still shunted the light of the new day as he squirmed out of the tent spluttering, attempting to remain quiet. Anna and Dieter stirred in their sleep. Crawling through the tents small port on hands and knees and onto the grass, he gasped for air—once, twice—before turning on his back to stare, wide eyed, at the blue-black sky above, punctured by a million stars.

Thrown together quickly the night before, sleeping in such a small makeshift space hardly wider for longer than a standing man, getting rest became untenable. With three full sized people sleeping there, the door thong tied shut, the air became stagnant and smelled of unwashed bodies and rancid clothes.

Neither did the conditions of the tent help him understand his continual claustrophoic condition that erupted over him many a night. Whatever ran in his veins, whatever shuddered in depths of his bloodied soul, it rarely allowed him rest—and on some days like this, it insisted on making itself known.

He expected the affliction to wear away in time—yet it still clung to him, like a shadow refusing to be shaken off. Moments of insanity often left him gasping when the memories of blood and guts surged upon him, vivid and unrelenting. Try as he might, he could not escape the din of spears screeching against shields, the cries of fallen men, or the acrid stench of the blood-soaked earth.

A mercilous silent war continued to be fought within the confines of his own mind. At times the conflict became so overwhelming he felt he might not achieve the next day. No name came to mind for this intense ill feeling, nor did he find need to name it. Closing his eyes, he tried to banish it again to that sunless cave in the back of his mind where memories went to sleep. He could lock it away in a box to be kept close in the far resses of his mind.

As the night slowly surrendered to the first blue streak that heralded the approaching dawn, Yakov's trembling breaths began to steady. He opened his eyes to again see the unyielding expanse of stars above, fewer now than before. Each point of light seemed to taunt him then blinked out to hide in the daylight. He sighed, sitting up to rub at his face. His hair now grown longer than in ages, touched his ears at the sides and tickled the back of his neck. His new, dark beard grew in uneven, bristling patches, gave accent to the dark circles that bruised the skin around his eyes.

After a creaking stretch, Yakov found himself wandering over to the edge of the clearing, intending to look out into the valley below. Surprised in this early flat light of dawn Yakov saw the silhouette of a figure hunched over and sitting on their haunches at the edge of the grassy knoll A cloak pulled tight around his bony shoulders, his hood thrown back, and thinning greasy hair ruffled slightly in the cold breeze sat their leader.

Suddenly cold himself, Yakov went to stand beside the figure.

"Father," he said simply.

"…Son," Hans Symon replied, looking at Yakov with age-old eyes. "Y'should be tossin' in sleep."

"As ought ye," Yakov smiled drily.

Der Flechtemann grunted, still looking out into the dark horizon as the sky brightened in bare increments.

"How is yer sister?" he asked after a pause.

Yakov sighed. "Unhappy, yet determined."

Hans smiled grimly. "Too much like me, then. For that is how I was—how a part o'me still is. Tell me," he turned to Yakov. "How…has yer life been?"

Yakov remained silent, unsure of what he should say. "It were fair and foul," he finally spoke, not looking at his father. "After ye departed, there was harmony among us siblings. The land offered solace during repetitive work. I found peace in the forests and the streams where I often disappeared. However, there were difficult times, stretching for days, weeks, and months. I believe my life be akin to any other life, equally filled with both blessings and hardships."

"You three are too mature for yer young years," the elderly man mumbled.

Yakov looked at him distantly, trying to find his own face in his father's, looking for the familiar wrinkles and contours. "Did ye have regrets?" he asked quietly.

36

"I told ye before," der Flechtemann said, his eyes flashing in defense as he looked up seeking Yakov's eyes. "I made mine choice, and I live with it."

"And ye shall not ask me of Karl? Yer brother?"

"He was always a fool. I simply realized not how *big* a fool."

Yakov laughed humorlessly. "And now, we shall set forthwith, nay lookin' back." Yakov eyed Hans suspiciously, a smirk on his face. "That would suit ye—then, ye could forget the guilt that chains yer neck so. Ye think that will answer the problem?" Yakov retorted. "Well, it does for a bit, for I carry my own guilt—but I understand now. I understand that I shall never escape the deeds I've seen or done. And father, neither will ye."

Der Flechtemann looked at him as though struck by his words—but it was only for a moment. As the first glimmer of the sun rose over the horizon, the mask of a rebel commander once more fell upon him. Yakov blinked and realized that Hans Symon once more disappeared behind the hood and beard his hair all ahoo. Only der Flechtemann stood before him now, rising with a grunt, immediately businesslike.

"Much needs doin'," he said to Yakov gruffly, looking around. "What did Sieg tell ye to do for today? Fetch water?"

"Nay," came Yakov's quick response. "Sieg's taking Anna and Dieter there for that. I'm to help cut the wood," Yakov said, quietly stepping back so more space buffered the affection between them. The vulnerable moment between father and son instantly disappeared.

Der Flechtemann nodded with deference. "See to that when the lads wake, then."

And with that injunction, he walked away, leaving Yakov standing at the edge, still watching the burnished crimson of treetops kiss the steel sky as first light tiptoed over the distant mountains, casting long shadows across the valley's dew-kissed grasses. Watching the land melt into strokes of pale saffron, Yakov thought of many things. Then, as the other rebels began to stir and crawl out of their own tents, he sighed and joined them, looking for an ax.

***

In the dappled sunlight in the heart of the valley, Anna and Dieter gathered their meager cloaks around themselves, pinning them in place with rusty brooches. They were about to embark on a short foraging expedition under Sieghart's watchful guidance. They would be setting snares, foraging for seasonal offerings, and collecting water from the stream. Anna, her flaxen hair tied back, exchanged a glance with Sieghart as they shared a rare moment of solitude beneath a bough, waiting for Dieter to fetch the snares.

"I'd like t'come along alone with ye," Anna said haltingly, "but it'd seem…"

"No, 'tis good," Sieg hurriedly said. "And besides, I promised yer Dieter I'd teach him a new snare."

She smiled, then frowned at Dieter as he arrived, his middle-parted dark hair falling into his eyes "Ye took yer time—is that everything?"

38

"Aye," Dieter said, sighing as he held up the buckets for her inspection. As she did so Anna could see, laying akimbo in the bottom, materials for the snares.

Satisfied, she looked at Sieg. "We're set t'go, then." Sieghart affirmed. Dieter dropped the bucket to his side. "Follow me, then," Sieg replied with a boyish grin as they set off. "Once y'know how to circle around fer the stream, ye two can show the others as well."

They trudged past der Flechtemann, who inspected the scout's equipment as the party passed. He shot a glance towards the trio, but said nothing. For her part, Anna ignored him entirely.

"We're headin' down to the stream," Anna called out to Yakov as she and Dieter walked towards the water and past his work. Her brother continued to chop wood, his hair plastered across his forehead, rivulets of sweat running down his wiry arms. He wiped sweat off his brow as he looked at her and nodded.

"Stay safe!" nodding at Dieter as if entrusting the responsibility of their sister's well-being to him; the youth nodded back, serious as ever.

She caught the glance almost immediately and scowled. "I can care for mineself," she snapped, storming to follow Sieghart. The older rebel, noticing Yakov's gaze, shrugged apologetically before leading Anna and Dieter out of camp.

"Yer hard on him," Sieghart said carefully as they walked. "'Tis natural fer him to worry."

"I know," Anna sighed, looking back as Dieter followed them at a leisurely pace, exploring his surroundings with curiosity. "Here, Dieter, don't ye tarry."

39

Dieter rolled his eyes but complied, hurrying his pace to match hers. "I'm nay infant," Dieter muttered darkly, but remembering Yakov's injunction, reluctantly fell into step with his sister. Quiet and introspective as always, he clutched the buckets with grimy hands, his expression inscrutable. Though his face, square-jawed and strong, retained much of his youth, yet marked by a certain greyish pallor. His hair had grown too long for Anna's liking, hanging down and plunging his eyes into a thoughtful shadow at times; however, even a quick glance could tell that his spirit was keen, far beyond his years.

"Y'need to trim yon locks," Anna said. Dieter only rolled his eyes.

They followed Sieghart's sprightly form, and twice Anna called to him, in exasperation, to slow down. His gait was naturally wide, his rugged figure bounced along the trail like a mummer in his dirt-worn green hose. On his shoulder, a sturdy bow rested strung, while a quiver of fletched arrows hung by a lanyard, attached top and bottom, across his back within easy reach of a grasp behind his head. With the confidence of a practiced woodsman, Sieg turned to Anna and Dieter, adjusting a faded black cap he wore over his fair locks.

"Stay close," he advised. "This valley be safe to my knowledge, aye, but each place has more t'offer than meets the eye. If there be some creature in contrary mood hidden smartly about, I'd rather not have ye chance upon it unawares."

Anna gave him an accusatory look. "Fine," she said as her hand swiped bruskly against her brother's shoulder. "Yer the one who keeps racin' afront, Sieg.

"Aye. And ye must race alongside me," Sieg retorted with a grin.

The trio navigated the path's strange twists and turns as they walked down the slop and rounded to the river, all the while guided by Sieghart's trail finding. In the past, while traveling with the band, Anna learned much about Sieg's life, but his skill as a scout and a reader of the terrain always surprised her. Anna looked at his back, wondering if this, too had been a skill learned from his father.

Sieghart, always tight-lipped about his father, grew up among a true travelling troupe—a childhood she believed enviable, though not a happy childhood from what little Sieg told her. Anna, through bits and pieces of casual conversation, gleaned his parents stole camp funds from the troupe while he was a boy and escaped with him in tow, only to have their stolen goods looted from them on the road. Unable to return and with nowhere else to go, they eked out a desperate existence as lone performers, travelling hamlet to hamlet. She still knew naught about what befell his parents—only he grew up scavenging to survive and taken up arms in a lance of mercenaries at some point before meeting der Flechtemann.

Along the way, Anna gathered wild herbs, nuts, and mushrooms into the hare skin satchel tied to her side, while Dieter's fingers worked to attempt to make a simple snare using some of the materials from one of the buckets and natural sticks and so near the path. He grew skillful at snaring small game over the years, and was thankful in his ability to carry his own weight,

"A valiant effort!" Sieghart said, gesturing for Dieter to walk over. "I notice ye have tried this before. Let's see how we might make a more successful snare for a brute of a cone." He chortled. "Let me get the drift of what ye have done here." Sieghart paused for a brief observation of what he held in his hands. After a bit of undescernable repetitive vocal sounds, low and to himself, he continued, "look here—follow mine hands as I fashion this one. I use the same as ye—twine and these pale, slender branches. But see how I tie the noose."

"It seems loose t'me," Dieter said doubtfully, but watching the elder friend carefully.

"For it is," Sieghart said easily, his eyes never leaving the task. "Can't make it too tight. If the twine wraps too tight, the creature shall struggle all the more. See here…?"

Dieter watched in agreement, focusing intently as Sieghart spoke. As the makeshift snare took shape, Dieter looked at the rebel friend of Anna's. "Thank ye," he finally spoke, his voice low. "I'll fashion one-such myself next time."

Sieghart gave him an encouraging smile. "I doubt ye not," he said, standing up to clap at his shoulder. "Ye'll make a fine hunter."

Dieter chuckled at that.

Anna, watching the exchange of comradery from a short distance away and smiled at the interaction. All too often, now, she would wonder at when circumstance would allow for her and Sieghart to marry—but she was glad, at least, the man she loved received welcome from her family. The thought of family, however, brought back the uncomfortable thought of her father… she shook her head as if to clear it.

"Well," Sieghart said, wiping his hands on his cloak. "Best keep our feet movin'. We're nearly there."

They quickly reached the tranquil stream, a pristine ribbon glistening under the gentle caress of sun. They wasted their hands and faces in the cool water, quenching their thirst. Then, alongside the babbling stretch of water, they filled not only the buckets but the waterskin Sieg carried with him from camp. The climb back along the widing trail with the added load was tiresome, but all three, now trim and in good shape, toughened over hard times, made their way quickly to camp and friends.

As the trio made their way back from the stream, they checked back on the snares, which Sieg earlier concealed carefully amidst the underbrush. Dieter noticed the first snare quivered in the bush, leaves rustling as if a whispered breeze blew by. With rare excitement, Dieter remarked to the other two. Sieg moved forward and carefully, leaned down to inspect the hidden noose. There, in the loop, they discovered their prize: a sleek, wild hare, its form quivering, exhausted, as it struggled half-heartedly to free itself from the restraint.

"Yer snare worked," he said to Sieghart. "Knife."

Sieg retrieved his short but heavy buthcher's knife from his belt, and made to dispatch the animal to prevent further suffering. Then hestitating, he looked to Anna for her trust. Realizing his intent, she paused, then slowly nodded to affirm the stroke, understanding the necessity and confirming the need. Many times came and went when she, too, could remember butchering animals for food. The act never presented a warm feeling on any occasion.

"Ye ought do it, Dieter. By yer own hand," Sieghart said, handing the knife to the young man. Nodding seriously, Dieter knelt near the animal with a deep breath. Definitely not the first animal he killed, but somehow this seemed to be

43

ceremonially significant. Sieg put a hand on Dieter's shoulder, nodding reassuringly.

"Thank ye," Dieter whispered in thanks to the hare. Then, mimicking the motion used by Anna, and Sieghart, and even him made in times past and present, he slew the animal with a quick, clean swipe of the sharp edge of the blade across the animals throat. The hare flailed and suddenly went still, and Dieter knew it was over.

"Cleanly done," Sieg said approvingly as Dieter released the hare from their snare.

With their catch secured, the siblings and Sieghart shared smiles, thankful for their good fortune. The trio carefully bundled the hare in a rag from Anna's satchel and headed back for camp.

***

They returned to an unwelcome surprise. At the entrance to their new camp, half a dozen strangers stood arguing with der Flechtemann, the rest of the rebels standing behind him with their weapons at the ready. Immediately, Sieghart braced himself for any unknown possibilities. Forming a clenched fist with his right hand and raising his arm he warned Anna and Dieter to stay put. Cautiously he walked up to the confrontation.

"Ho, there!" he called. "What's afoot here?"

The apparent leader of the strangers turned around to look at Sighart with unfriendly eyes. A tall, frayed old man with stirngs of matted grey hair falling around a pruned, red-hued face stood before the assembled body.

44

"Well, they say 'tis their clearin'," der Flechtemann said in a composed tone of voice.

"Since when do namless clearings become property for the likes of any of us?" Sieg frowned at the newcomers, noting their bows and arrows, and their deerskin cloaks. "Hunters, are ye?"

"Me fathers," the tattered old man said in a scratching, rasping growl. "I've been tracking game 'ere abouts since I been unable to see over the dale's tall grass. These trees ha'e been me sustenance since I be naught but a suckling babe, friend! I nay ken ye to stake a claim on what's rightly ours."

"We apologize," der Flechtemann said, raising a placatory hand. "Fer we were unaware of yer folk and yer ways. We intend t'stay only for a few days, and yer welcome t'camp beside us."

"I trust ye nay a bit," the man said bluntly. "These are times of ill feeling, and ye may bring blight to our valley, an unpleasant canker we canna abide. This aside, I don't like the look o' ye. For sure yer an unsavory lot, clearly a-fleein'— what ye be? Brigands?"

"If we were brigands," Sieg said hotly, stepping forward, "Ye wouldn't have a tongue left between yer teeth."

The old man glowered a rye squint at Sieghart before looking at der Flechtemann. "Nay, I do'na ken ye. Leave."

Behind der Flechtemann, one of the younger partisans laughed. "Wha' ye sayin' old man? I suppose ye'll make us go?"

Der Flechtemann turned around immediately, looking for who to admonish, but the old man was already frothing.

"Ye challenge me with yer sharpened weapons…yer bows knocked towards us…and think me weak?" he hissed, seething as he stamped the earth with his foot. Rising to a howling screech the old man fought to control the emotional retort of the moment. "Keep yer willful threats, and I'll give thee something far better fer to worry. Here, I curse ye—I curse ye in the name of me long line of fathers, in the name of me dead brothers with whom I suckled. Stay, and may ye be buried on this hill!"

Spitting on the floor between them, the old man turned away, walking off with the other hunters behind him.

As they left, Sieghart conferred with der Flechtemann, while Yakov pushed through the throng of chattering members of the partisan camp to take the water buckets from Anna and Dieter who stood watching the commotion from the edge of the camp.

"What make ye of that?" Dieter muttered. "A curse?"

"There's no such thing, so worry not," Yakov said, sounding unconvinced in his own words.

As they headed back to their camp site, the rebels thronged about the center of the clearing where a council, of sorts, convened around their leader. After the water was safely collected and covered, the siblings sat on the periphery of the meeting, while der Flechtemann, Sieghart, Nerijus, Elias, and other important division leaders sat around a fire to discuss happenings which transpired only a short while before.

Elias' voice, low but firm, spoke, "I ken y'wish to be reasonable, but we can't ignore blatant truth—the fact is these folk want us gone. They hath no loyalty to us or any, and, as well, they clamber up and down the mountains speakin' of the old rights, claimin' this and that as it suits 'em. Then they trudge, hands out, to the towns, they claim to hate, every season to sell their bounty. They are godless folk, and I trust them not."

"What's God t'do with it?" Nerijus scoffed. "Now, I ken yer concern, to an extent. They may come upon that fiend, the Chain, on our trail…"

"And lead him exactly here," der Flechtemann muttered, deep in thought.

Sieg nodded as well. "On this, I agree with Elias. There minds were only intent on ill-will towards us."

"We could parley," Nerijus offered. "I'm not suggestin' we trust 'em, but we might do better t'make them understand we're not the enemy. They were wary of us 'cuz we were unclear of our intent."

Der Flechtemann looked intently at Nerijus. "Yer right, in a way. If time were with us, we could explain our struggle aligns with theirs. The mercenaries dogs on our trail are workin' for an order, which will, in time, ruin these folks own old ways of livin'. Bein' in agreement betwixt them and us, and with them showin' a whit of willingness to do so, something could be done, but time is not on our side."

"And wha' be our offer t'them to ensure their silence?" Elias asked, casting a disdainful glance at Nerijus. "Nay, we possess nay riches, all scattered as it is. Nay, my friend—I ken ye are inclined to trust swiftly, but I be not, nay. Even if they do'na stumble upon the Chain's trail themselves—imagine what they might do once they return to a village? They'll speak loudly and disapprovingly of our presence. Our adversary is'na merely the Chain, but every arrogant corrupt noble. Who's t'say some scoundrel knight flashing a coat of arms will'na come to round us up? Before long, we'd find ourselves confined and paraded to the gallows."

Nerijus pursed his lips, clearly still not in agreement..

The rebel leader stroked his graying beard in deep thought, the lines of age creating dark shadows over his brow. "Curse it all, but Elias speaks truth. Seems t'me diplomacy remains the luxury of king-folk and dukes, while we are given nay an option." Der Flechtemann stood and announced with final determination, "We must break camp and head out tomorrow at dawn."

A smattering of groans could be heard across the attentive group as the announcement came and the camp dispersed to their tents for one more night of sleep. The last few nights of rest brought a welcome reassured rest to the camp. Now, with the threat of discovery motivating them, the nomadic partisans made their plans to move once more.

Yakov exchanged a look with Dieter.

"I take it back," he sighed, dismayed. "The curse seems t'have worked, after all."

Chapter IV: Morgenlicht

"The Seeker breathes between moments, and each moment is a breath of the path; each cobble is a face to be read, and each face is a step forth...[and] what man may know what the morrow brings? What man may know what hides in the dawn?"

-Brother Jakob, circa 1383

It took days of near-sleepless travel to cross the valley. In the midday's light the siblings trudged listlessly, their feet to calloused and furrowed with cuts and bruises, to swollen for their shoes. The smooth, worn-out soles made walking a chore and balance from the pain in each step made the trek even more difficult. Falling became commonplace in the drudgery of each movement. This became especially noticeable when walking alongside the narrow, rocky paths carved along the stony walls were pocked with cairns within which a person could severely sprain and ankle or take a wicked tumble down a rock embankment. Scrapes, cuts, and bruises became resident nuisances on each traveler.

Near the edge of the valley, they finally came across signs of civilization. The scouts, sent by der Flechtemann at the beginning of the day, returned with news of a hamlet not far from their current location, there apprehensive nature became apparent as they spoke to der Flechtemann, however. As, Hans, the old rebel and Sieghart sat deep in thought, Yakov hesitantly approached.

"Is all well?" he asked.

Sieg pointed in the direction from which the scouts came as he spoke, "These two come across a small hamlet named Morgenlicht a few twists and turns that-a-way. Them fields of the village should look more cared for, they said, but they ain't. According to our scouts, hardly any people t'were seen, and the one old woman givin' the chance to talk to seemed crazy as the wind in the trees. She made nay since. Spooky as t'was they found nay reason t'run,… but somethin' mighty queer seemed afoot.

"Aye, I ken yer worries, but we've got t'give it a go," declared der Flechtemann. "We canna' survive on boiled pinecones, stripped of their seeds, and tough old hare, nay even the wild dogs would touch that. If for nothin' else, we need t'let our feet and horses rest. The animals are weary, and the mules are cryin' out for some respite."

"What if it be a trap?" Yakov asked, his mind's eye flashing with the Chain's wicked grin.

"Then we must chance it," der Flechtemann grimly said, before looking at Yakov cryptically. "When we arrive at the outskirts, ye and I shall go into the village."

Why me? Yakov thought.

Evidently, he was not alone in this thought. From behind them, Elias spoke, arms crossed, "I esteem thee, der Flechtemann," he said in his low gravely voice. "But I know nay yer son too well. I would hesitate t'entrust yer life to 'im."

"I carry my life in mine own hands," the rebel leader said, the dart of his flashing eyes leveled at Elias. "Same as any man."

"Yet thine life is most precious t'the cause,… more than ye may know," Elias evenly replied, standing firm, not

50

backing down from his leaders stern focus. With conciliation he continued, "I shall bring my bow."

In the world, some men do not bend—men with faith so complete, with such certainty in their mind, they would do the unthinkable for their belief. Elias, Yakov surmised, was such a man—utterly dedicated to his father and the cause of the commoner, being inhumanly loyal, to the point of insufferability.

"Very well," der Flechtemann finally agreed with a frown, turning to Yakov. "Ye send word down the line, lad. We make fer Morgenlicht."

***

The hamlet came into sight early the next day as the partisans trekked through the valley and down a sloping trail. In the distance, the village lay serene with the far off backdrop of rugged Alps mountains like the wings of great angels. Dawn's first light shimmered in dappled streaks through the dark clouds of almost-winter, and Yakov understood why the village would have been named Morgenlicht—morning light. Here, there was open sky and open land, prepared coyly for the sun's kiss.

Yet a specter of gloom hung about the ramshackle aspect of the village. Squat cottages, constructed from dark timber and unyielding stone, gave no smoke, sloping fields lay desolate even at this hour.

"Be safe," Anna muttered to Yakov, looking distrustfully at the hamlet in the distance. "It seems a sour place. Something be wrong there."

51

The rebel leader strode up and mounted the grey Andalusian, before looking down at Yakov. "Can ye ride?" he asked.

"Not well," Yakov admitted. True as it was, the closest he came to mounting any horse was when he and his fellow soldiers took turns on a skittish mare, a beast taken from a local merchant in lieu of his debt. During the entirety of his service, Yakov, a part of the common levy, remained untrained in riding—the mare, he remembered, bucked him off without ceremony, then snorted away, his partners in the affair laughing and cavorting while the horse bested all of them in turn.

"Y'need learnin', then. We shall share a beast fer now," der Flechtemann said, and feeling slightly sheepish, Yakov climbled up behind him on the the tall grey's hind quarters.

"There, there Wolke. Settle now. Easy, easy." der Flechtemann patted the steely neck of the strong horse and combed at the silky main with strong fingers as his mount continued its complaint at the extra weight. "I know there be good grit in thine hooves. Can ye not bear this wisp of a lad?"

As if affronted at the suggestion, the horse quieted. Der Flechteman gave a rare chuckle, and they were off. Behind them, Elias followed at a muted trot on his freckled mare, a strangely curved bow hoisted on his shoulder.

"He wears a strange bow," Yakov muttered looking at it.

"A fine weapon—yew if I am not mistaken, fashioned in the style of the horse-folk," der Flechtemann said, glancing at the bow. "I know not how he came across it, but it be a fine bow fer taking a mounted shot—more compact, less unwieldy in a saddle."

52

"Archery from horseback?" Yakov asked, trying to wrap his mind around the idea. "A strange feat."

"And a good trick t'know," der Flechtemann said as they rode along. "I know the bones o' the skill, learnt frem the Bulgars. The old 'uns of their clans still know the practice. Are ye fascinated by the bow as well, son?"

"Perhaps—I've not thought much of it," Yakov admitted. "Conscripts such as I were spearmen, one and all, lowly fodder t'be chafed on the frontlines."

Der Flechtemann contracted his parched lips in a silent grin, welcoming the chance to work more with his son, now grown to a man, he assumed he may never see again. "Then we shall teach ye o' the bow, as well,… in time." He said.

Soon, they were entering the hamlet riding among the quiet huts and homes, window openings black without animation of life. The glow of the morning sun, beautiful in the distance, created eerie shadows over unkempt thatch roofs. Here and there unsightly mud daub chunks lay on the ground near walls where they fell leaving chinks in the walls of huts for lack of attention. To this unsightliness a sickly odor rose from someplace in the rubble.

"A foul place," Elias said, looking around as they trotted towards what in better times would have been the main square.

The public square was a grimy affair, muddied by time, dwarfed by an ancient oak tree as its gnarled branches invoked unspoken questions. As they cantered through the half-light, they took in the suffering that enveloped the town. A fragile tranquility now settled over the place, as if the world itself held its breath. Charred poles were driven into the dirt. casting further long, wavering shadows on the

53

dilapidated homes. Der Flechtemann's eyes darkened to see the blackened stakes. Sickened by the carnage, Yakov could invision ther use. The faint scent of charred timber and flesh still lingered in the crisp morning air. He knew the work of the Chain.

A slim, muddy stream slithered through the settlement, reflecting a mercurial glint in the dawn. There, the rebels first found signs of the villagers—a bony trio of women were washing clothes in the water as two men sat by a fire some distance behind them. As the rebels neared, the women looked at them with wide, alarmed eyes, while the men stood up hesitantly, holding makeshift clubs in shaking hands.

Der Flechtemann and the others dismounted. As Elias took their horses to tie them to the tree, Yakov and the rebel leader walked towards the villagers.

As they slowly approached the group gathered at the water's shore, der Flechtemann stroked his shaggy beard, his gravelly voice quiet, he muttered in Yakov's hearing, "Stay close and speak not. I must know what befell yon defeated lot—yet if things go ill, ye must sprint fer the horse."

Yakov nodded as they continued to move cautiously toward the small gathering of locals. The villagers' faces bore the pallid glare of suffering, their eyes brimming with tales of hardship and loss. Der Flechtemann first approached one of the women, an ancient-looking person, her wrinkled cheeks driven hollow into her face.

"Mornin' to ye, mother," der Flechtemann began, inclining his head. "We come frem a troupe o' men, mummers and the like, encamped at the far edge of this hamlet. We came fer supplies—yet what ill has befallen this town? Why does suffering grip at ye?"

54

The woman regarded him suspiciously, her eyes filled with doubt as she fixed her gaze on their weapons. "Soldiers for hire, they did. Not but a moon's turn past, they came lookin' for them rebels." She spoke hoarsely, her voice reminiscent of a morning fog. "They laid waste to our cottages, took our victuals. Our lasses can't even nurse their young 'uns. They all be dyin' of hunger and cold.

Yakov's heart grew heavy with regret. He knew instantly this deed was the vicious work of the Chain. Many a time as a conscript he and Mikkel, his once mercenary friend, traveled from farmstead to farmstead seeking provision for the knight's army. Requisitioning grain and goods as well as demanding tribute were only a portion of their duties. They, however, never were required to stay behind to see the aftermath or devastation the army caused as it tramped onward. The worst part at this moment, of course, was Yakov knew this hunt focused on *their party.* The hardship brought to these people was the focus of the Chain's hunt for the rebel band.

"Their leader," he said in a faint voice, stepping forward as though not by his own will. "What be he like?"

Der Flechtemann shot him a warning look. The woman hesitated, her gaze darting between der Flechtemann and Yakov. "Ye don't strike me as mummers." The old woman paused for a moment. Then her eyes widened in recognition, "Them sort don't carry bows. Valdi? Valdi, come here!"

One of the men approached, his gaze, too, flitting between the rebels. "Why do ye trouble my mother?" he called in a faltering voice.

"We mean no ill," der Flechtemann said, putting a rough hand on Yakov's shoulder. Yakov started, as if suddenly waking up.

"We don't care who ye are," the other man called, his voice harsh. "Mercenary, rebel…whatever. We don't care for ye."

"Wait!" the old woman squinted at der Flechtemann. "Have ye food? At yer camp—what food have ye?"

And with the woman's command and request, der Flechtemann found himself back in control as he strided forward, arms in clear sight so as not to alarm the villagers. His chin was held up, the aura of a great leader returning. Warmth radiated from his eyes, and Yakov felt somenting new in the awe of this person, der Flechtemann. Now in his heart rose a desire to follow this man who walked on the earth like a myth from an old tale.

"I have naught enough stores t'share as is," he began, but in his baritone voice, comforting, peaceful, and even, he continued. "Yet an idea has settled to me mind. Mother and friends, I lay a trade before ye. Me and mine lot are tired from walkin' through this valley. Our feet ache somethin' fierce and chafe with sores. To that we nay rest in many nights. Should ye allow us some space—space to rest, space to breathe, I shall send our archers and trappers down into yon valley t'procure more game. I have, too, folk well-versed in herb skills fer healin', and we shall see to yer ills. First we take care of yer young—as though they were our own, I swear ye this."

"We already sent our menfolk into the valley," the old woman said. "But game there is more than scarce as the weather grows poor from winter's creep the animals have gone to ground. We reasoned even with the huntin' valley-men who have lived there of ages past, half-heathen though they be. But ever since…the *cullin'* here in our small village, they refuse t'trade with us. They are down-spirited folk, and fear we shall pass our curse of poor luck to them."

"We stand before ye as proof o'the skill of our folk," der Flechtemann said. "We shall aid yer hungry, mother, at least for the coming few days. I swear this to thee."

The villagers stepped back and conferred for a moment. Distrustful glances continued to be shot towards Yakov. Elias stood quietly in the shadows, his bow arm deceptively relaxed.

"I told ye to speak not," der Flechtemann muttered to Yakov.

"I know," Yakov replied in a low voice. "I needed only t'know if—"

"Hello… old man," called Valdi, the son of the elderly woman, stepping forward. "We agree to yer terms fer now, but ye must not bring any weapons here. Ye can take turns restin'. We won't inquire 'bout yer identity, but yer fate will be in your own hands."

"Der Flechtemann half-bowed in assent, hand pressed to his chest in a local show of gratitude. As the haggard villagers looked at them with concern in their faces, the rebels re-mounted.

"Elias," der Flechtemann said, "Ride ahead. Tell the folk what ye have heard. Yakov and I shall return in time."

Elias nodded, though he looked none too happy at the thought. As he rode away, der Flechtemann and Yakov trotted slowly through the hamlet, navigating through the cloying stench and past darkened houses, each corner revealing more signs of anguish. As villagers glanced fearfully from windows or huddled around fires, der Flechtemann would wave at them and exchange a few words. A tired-eyed woman, clutching a hungry child, spoke of her brother's abduction by the marauders. An old man, bearing the weight of age, cried as he spoke of their lost livestock, sniffling too much to be understood much further.

Yakov's head throbbed at the misery around him, and he could almost see the weight of desperation pressing down on der Flechtemann. The man seemed to grow older in his saddle, his back more bent, a single finger on his hand twitching.

"Y'see why I fight?" he suddenly asked.

"Aye," Yakov said quietly, feeling his father's hunched back, beginning to stoop with age, as he sat behind him on the horse. "But the Chain did this for our sake. If no rebellion, this lot would nay have suffered."

Der Flechtemann half-turned in the saddle. "There was no rebellion in the lands yer mother ran from. Yet she suffered all o' this and worse. There be always a reason, boy, when it comes t'the sufferin' of the common—and the reason is that they be common."

Yakov was quiet for a while, then spoke. "What d'ye mean, of mother?"

"What does ye know?"

"I know mother came from the lands o' the 'Rus," Yakov said, his mouth dry as the visages of his mother flashed before his eyes, her gaze unblinking, her hair hanging in listless threads. "I know she ran from servitude, ye found and married her."

"They beat her," der Flechtemann said bluntly with little emotion. "The wealthy lords of her land were the same as the lords of mine. They murdered her pa and brothers, subjected her ma to unspeakable horrors, and beat yer mother so severely she could scarcely utter a word. War erupted after, as one agile young lord killed another. Suddenly, the fields, ablaze, blackened beyond use, her master was no more—she fled that very night. A year from that same moment, I discovered her. And that should'ave been the end of it."

"But it wasn't, nay?" Yakov asked, dreading the answer.

"'Twas the way they abused her," his father grunted abruptly, "Took me a good while to reckon, albeit must've been the root of it. She lost her wits with time. She could still work the farm w'me, but then, first, she'd nay ken things—trifles, aye, but after, more serious, she'd forget 'bout you young 'uns. Leavin' ye in the house alone t'fend for yer'selves. She forgot my name in time. Forgot to tend the hearth one day 'til we near 'bout turned to cinders—all when Dieter were but a babe, ye a bit older and Anna not much older still. I s'pose she figured Anna could take care o'ye, but Anna be only six or so at the time. 'Twas then I began to understand—her body I could hold, but nay her spirit. I'd lost her, just like so much else, to the whims of them wretched lords and princes."

"And yet, ye could've cared fer her. Ye *ought* t'have cared fer her. Yet ye ran," Yakov said, hot tears running down his cheeks in streams, now focused on der Flechtemann's face, his hurt reflected in his eyes with accusation. A part of him wished he could strike his father. He sought to avenge himself and his mother and his siblings upon this man who now sat in the saddle, trying to placate his son, head humbled in admonition.

"I..." der Flechtemann began, then went silent. Quietly, he turned his horse and began the journey back to camp. Nothing more could be said. Time would have to heal the misunderstood void between the two.

***

Yakov, raising his arms akimbo stretched, then winced as sore muscles from travel cramped his back. The thatched barn offered shelter but afforded little resembling comfort. Bales of coarse straw and moldy hay allowed makeshift beds, while wooden walls riddled with gaps barely kept out the biting night air.

The siblings and their fellow rebels entered the village around midday. Yakov remembered how whispered conversations filled narrow streets. The villagers, their faces gaunt and long-suffering, watched the newcomers with a wary eye. Der Flechtemann's words might have won them, but in a world marked by betrayal and cruelty, trust became a fragile commodity. The first hunting party led by Sieg and Nerijus set off around the same time, and they would likely be returning the next day—hopefully with plentiful game.

For now, Anna, Yakov, and Dieter huddled together for warmth and security, their faces grimy and worn with weariness. Dieter seemed to have fallen asleep almost instantly as he tended to, his hand nestled in the crook of his arm. Around the barn, other rebels snored or tossed and turned. A pair of legs was even dangling from the rafters.

60

In a whispered voice, Yakov told Anna about the exchange between their father and him. After this, silence encombered their thoughts for a moment until her countenance changed and she focused through Yakov with far-away eyes.

"I had forgotten the fire," she said softly.

"He said you were only little," Yakov said, his mind still churning. "I knew mine mother must have suffered…but what he tells me breaks my soul. May God send pestilence upon such folk," he said bitterly, trying not to think of his mother as a young woman, fleeing through the night with a bloodied forehead, eyes wide.

"Sufferin's the lot of so many—in each village, each corner o' Christendom, the same sufferin' repeats," Anna whispered, her voice trembling, "Does ye understand now? This is why I believe in this cause."

"I see it clearer now," Yakov said, eyes shut. "And mayhaps I am a fool—but I see it clear."

Anna paused, looking at him intently. "Does ye believe as well… now?"

Yakov, staring into the distance, his mind a turbulent sea of thoughts, turned his gaze to his sister. Darkness hid the features of his face with the exception of bare lines of exhaustion caught by the dim glow of the moon from a window. He hesitated for a moment, then nodded slowly.

"Yes," he said, his voice barely audible. "I believe."

Anna's eyes widened. She despised her father for the pain he brought to them, but she held onto the hope the cause, at least, could bring about change. She reached out to

61

clasp Yakov's hand, her grip both warmly comforting and eminently reassuring.

The weight of Yakov's decision hung heavily in the air, and Anna needed to know more. "Tell me, my little Yakov," she urged softly, "Was it but the truth about mother that swayed yer mind?"

"Nay," Yakov's voice quavered, then grew steadier as he spoke. "I've seen…sufferin'. Such sufferin' of the common folk, Anna. Not just here, but this whole time, I have *seen*. Was I not the Chain's field-dog fer a time? I tore chainmail from the dead, still clogged with corpse-hair…I…I marched with a godless man's godless levy, and I knew the cruelty mine spear comitted. The corruption and cruelty of this false order, I see it, Yet I could not bear t'see, Anna—so I looked away. I looked away and away, but today—when it was mother—I could look away no longer."

Yakov realized his cheeks were wet, though his voice seemed certain. Before him, Anna nodded, her eyes glistening in the darkness with barely contained tears. "Ye knows I've believed in this cause from the start, even if…that man's actions rankle at me. But I see as well as ye, Yakov. We cannot let the sufferin' o' the folk people go unanswered. 'Tis as Sieg says—the cycle of corruption must stop."

Dieter, awakened in the midst of their conversation, his sleepiness giving way to curiosity. As the whispering continued, he finally looked up at his siblings with mild irritation. "What's afoot?" he asked.

Yakov turned to Dieter, his gaze exhausted. "Naught of much value to thee or anyone else, brother of mine. We speak talkin' about the rebellion. And I believe…that I believe, I s'pose."

62

Dieter gave him a measured look, then sighed. "And that's well enough for thee—but ye needs rest… and so do I. So sleep!"

With this, their youngest brother turned over and slipped into quiet snoring. Anna and Yakov shared a silent chuckle—and the mirth of a moment. The two talked until the moon no longer shown in the night's sky. Anna slipped into sleep first. Their sharing replaced the respite from the weight of the world, but Yakov's night remained sleepless. The first early glow of dawn began to make its lazy appearance over the mountains in the east as Yakov finally nodded, eyes shutting for what slumber may be left.

Chapter V: Sacrifice

"All causes demand sacrifice—and what use is sacrifice, if not for the right cause?."

-Brother Jakob, circa 1383

In the days that followed, the rebels dedicated themselves to fulfilling their obligations to the village, venturing into the valley in relentless shifts. They hunted game, gathered bounties of the wild, and foraged for whatever sustenance could be plucked from the cold earth. The hard-fought battle against the elements, reminded every rebel of the suffering this settlement accepted for the sake of helping these foreign men, women, and children—now, a sense of loyalty pushed the band of patriots to their limits, reinforced with the stern sermons of der Flechtemann and the other senior 'officers' of the assembled like Nerijus and Elias.

But their sorties into the valley were not without challenges. Standoffs with the local hunters immediately became a frequent occurrence, with warning arrows loosed on both sides. With winter fast approaching, the valley-men remained reluctant to share their resources with the rebels. Their desire to defend personal territory was strong, stronger than any sentiment to help their fellow man.

Tensions continued to simmer beneath the surface, ready to ignite at any moment. Without exception, winning the hunters' trust and ensuring a steady flow of game into the village was the only long-term solution. Yet the hunter-folk saw the rebels as interlopers and the villagers as ill omens. The conflict between them threatened to reach a boiling point.

Elias and Sieg both chafed at the delay, reminding der Flechtemann that the Chain was assuredily close on their trail—but the rebel leader remained unmoved, determined to bring some degree of solace, no matter how temporary to the inhabitants of this hamlet.

"They shall suffer heartilty worse should the Chain follow us here," Elias argued. "'Tis no kindness to these folk fer us t'tarry."

To these frequent outbursts from his advisors, der Flechtemann would not respond. His undivided mind now firmly set on the affair at hand, a genuine benevolence flickered in his eyes given freely to the village peoples and the hunters of the hills. Yakov watched him from afar, his heart in conflict—how could such a man be so filled with empathy? A man who left his own family, yet seemed to care for each common man the same, a man who appeared so distant and cold and cruel, a man willing to lie and steal and kill—how could such a man be so willing show so much good?

The fourth day in the village, Sieghart's hunting party, just returned, panting and wild-eyed, dragged, not just a half-butchered deer behind them, but an injured rebel, glassy eyed and sputtering in pain. His jaw set, Sieghart reported to der Flechtemann as the old rebel, hearing the commotion, appeared before his hut.

"Them louse-ridden dogs have done it this time," Sieg said in unrestrained irritation. "Another volley of warnin' arrows exchanged while we were skinning yon beast—but they stopped nay at warnin' this time. The second volley aimed squarely fer our throats, though we made it all, 'cept him. They be cheap folk, and if the Chain be not already bitin' our ankles, that nest of vermon shall bring him to us unbidden."

"I hear ye m'friend—cool yer head," Der Flechtemann acknowledged with a worrisome frown, before gesturing to the other rebels. Their leader turned with determination in his stance. "Ye lot, see to our man—give him what ye can, and call Werner. See if he hath a poultice of some kind."

As the rebels busied themselves, a decision was made—the band would have to leave the village soon. Moving once again to find safety. Noticeably, even the few days of help brought the settlement in close comradarie to the partisons. Yakov and his siblings, discouraged at having to move once again, moved slowly with obvious reluctance as they took count of the rations and began the arduous process of packing. Food, spread out thinly amongst all, with barn rats a constant menace and rueful foe in a survival fight. Through all this the locals kept a nervous though hopeful eye on the rebels. In what seemed an eternity of migration, this rest constituted the best, the only welcome rest for the group, a safe haven to be cherished. Only now relations began to thaw between the villagers and the partisans. Yet now, they would again have to march on. Anna cooked her last stew for the village-folk as they waited with hopeful eyes, and Yakov understood the warmth with which she interacted with them. She would miss helping these people, he knew.

But farewells were a familiar song and dance to Yakov, who least associated the with the villagers and for this very reason. A childhood and adulthood spent on the road or in garrisons taught him not to make attachments with the locals—nothing lasted long enough to put down roots or make a corner his own. His things remained in a neat pile constantly, ready to be whisked up at a moment's notice—yet he saw a certain distance in Dieter's face, even more so than usual. His younger brother now a friend to several of the young men of the village watch. They shared several good moments and celebrations together only to have to part so suddenly.

"How long can we run?" Dieter muttered incoherently, bitter with spite, as he loaded another mass of supplies into the back of one of the wagons. "We split wood t'wood piles like fools."

Yakov looked at him quietly, not knowing what to say. "Ye ought t'have grown used to it by now," he finally said.

"In a way, I have. Yet I fear," Dieter said, looking at Yakov with a confused glance. "I fear what this life is. I fear thee and I and our sister shall end up as naught but wraiths, goin' place t'place fer nay reason, with nay a place t'call home."

With that, Dieter returned to the preparations as Yakov remained lost in thought, his brother's words tumbling over and over through his mind. He returned to his own chores, and by nightfall, everything was prepared. The next morning, they would leave Morgenlicht behind.

As they tried to sleep in the barn, Yakov stayed awake hearing the snores of the tired rebels and the sniffling of the wounded man. Outside, an owl hooted in a solitary moan, while the odd insect hummed in the far underbrush, as if singing a final chorus before the onset of winter killed it. No dogs barked—with grim certainty, Yakov knew the starving villagers must have made quick work of them.

67

With the hunger of thousands of people in the Empire weighing on his mind, Yakov could not sleep. He tossed and turned, the beginnings of a terrible suggestion coiling in his mind. The thought did not present anything new though he dreaded its implication with dread. Being pursued now proved to exact a terrible toll on the partisans' efforts to find safety. The enemy grew closer than ever with each passing day, and not knowing the Chain's mind became a source worry for all. Exhausted scouts could no longer continue to reliably run back and forth between the charging mercenaries and the fleeing rebels....Too, conceivably, pockets of the Chain's men sighted roving this far south months ago, indicated he could be planning something entirely unexpected as a possible trap for the band of rebels. The fear of what the future may hold was too great to dismiss.

Now, with his heart cold, Yakov stood up, careful not to wake Anna or Dieter as he carefully tip-toed, stepping over and around them, passing by the tangle of sleeping limbs. He creaked through the an door, and crept past sleeping village houses, where—for the first time in ages—peasants slept with a morsel of nourishment in their bellies. He walked past rebel sentries and scrawny lads from the local watch, nodding at them in turn, before making his way to the main square. There, under a great tree, der Flechtemann's tent now protected, a welcoming open pavilion under which the old leader sat, eyes shut. They flicked open as Yakov's feet crunched on the loose earth.

"Yer awake," Yakov said.

"My sleep is rare," der Flechtemann replied, the gravel in his tired voice. "Two hours or three—they all be the same. Why do ye come t'me at this hour, son?"

Yakov stood before the grizzled man, and took a deep breath.

"I have a plan."

***

Long days lengthened into two weeks as the rebels inched south toward the Alps, their hearts heavy with the constant threat of the Chain and his band of mercenaries. Narrow trails snaked upwards into the mountains, barely wide enough for a single person to pass. Many were nigh invisible, markled only by stony cairns built by earlier travelers. The ground beneath their worn soles was treacherous, strewn with dusted snow, loose rocks, and hidden crevices that threatened to send them skidding down the deceptively gentle-seeming slopes. Each step was precarious, requiring a steady nerve.

The intensity of the pursuit increased at an alarming rate. The rare scout the group of partisans could afford to dispatch to watch repeated the same news: the Chain gained ground daily, shortening the distance between the two groups. Low, distant howls, echoing through the desolate, stony hillside, accompanied by the Chain's men as they moved, created uneasiness in the rebel band, who, shivering in the cold and unable to rest, passed the night in stressful sleeplessness.

"Hounds," Sieghart said grimly.

Remembering the sound now, Yakov shivered; during his short stint as a conscript in the Chain's band, he witnessed firsthand the brutal efficiency with which the leader could employ war dogs in the mercenary operations. The hounds, bred and trained specifically for combat by enterprising kennel masters, were useful for any band of independent operators. Yakov remembered their scarred,

69

muscular bodies and yellowing teeth all too well. The Chain bought them occasionally from his contacts, only selecting the strongest and most aggressive breeds. The beasts would be fed scraps to keep them hungry and fierce. Of course, often being over aggressive brought forward the constant need to put them down, they never lived long, which required them to be replaced seasonally. Too, in a rare instance the dogs were killed by those targets they pursued. Generally, because of the temperament, the dogs became too frantic to handle.

Yakov, in the service of the Chain, witnessed the hounds in action many times. They moved with brutish precision. Their senses finely attuned to the scent of their prey. Trained to track, immobilize, and kill, they added a lethal, unrelenting force to their master's arsenal. If the hounds held the scent of a target, little escape prevailed. For Yakov's plan, by a stroke of luck, the scouts gave a report sighting a stream a short distance ahead—a stream he could use as a hinge element for his plan to work.

In the shadow of the towering peaks, the rebels took a short rest now amidst the rocky outcrops and dense thickets, catching their breaths. Dirt-smeared rebel scouts perched among the stones, lest the band be taken by surprise. Under an outcrop not far from the old hunting trail the band of rebels followed, Dieter and Anna blew into their hands, with alternate periods of time placing them in the pits of their arms trying their hardest to keep warm.

As Dieter looked around, he noticed Yakov attentively stood near their father. Dieter frowned, he noticed ever since leaving Morgenlicht Yakov spent much of his time in der Flechtemann's company speaking in low tones, sometimes looking around at others in the group or off into the distance.

The plans Yakov and der Flechtemann made continued to be secretive. To that, Dieter felt uncomfortable not knowing what would come. Being one of the youngest of age to fight, he did not fully appreciate Yakov's rise in authority after serving in the Chain's army only a short time ago, and did not know whether to fully trust him or not. Too, the recent discovery der Flechtemann may be his brother and sister's father, shocked them all; however, he felt little towards the strange man. Though Hans Symon may be his father, their interactions were short and distant, and as far as Dieter was concerned, he'd gotten along well enough knowing der Flecthemann as the leader of the group and not as their father—the unveiling of a father now, as it were, mattered little. Der Flechtemann and Sieghart's teaching over the last short years taught Dieter much about survival in the wild. *He could not remember those years ago when der Flechtemann may have been his father… anyway,* Dieter thought.

"Damn this cold," came a mutter. Dieter looked to see it came from Nerijus huddled nearby. His nose bitterly red, glowed like a bruised apple. "O, I'd lost mine remembrance o'this bite…" the rebel complained. "My bones are drawn brittle in this pale hell."

"'Tis a bitter cold, aye," Anna shivered. "Friend Nerijus—how far is the enemy?"

Nerijus, weary from no sleep, looked passively towards the siblings and sighed with tired resignation. "In the day past, me and me sentries climbed an overlook outcrop much like this—there behind us," he said pointing over his shoulder. "T'the north, the enemy's camp… sits there. Bright red standards flew in this devil-wind, and men like black ants swarmin' in the light cast by flecks o' fire. We lay there low 'pon our empty bellies and wondered at their strength o' numbers. Twice, if nay more, the number of lances our folk vanquish'd last we met the Chain's lot. He 'as won for himself right favor from the bishop's and the noble's cretin scum—those with wealth taken from the likes o' ye and me who now finance and give writ to his evil force." He shook his head slowly, looking into the fire before him. "Far be it from me to cast doubt upon thy father's intentions, but I fear for our skins."

Anna grew quiet with little left to add. Faith, hope, despair, misery, all such things were now eclipsed by the sheer exhaustion setting into their bones. Their minds grew numb to the surroundings of cold and no shelter, and the desperate happenings presented to them in reports from Nerijus. Even the respite of a hot meal as they scrambled, crack-lipped and sore-limbed, from a threat that seemed to be closing in at every moment, could be afforded the band.

Around them, the air was thin and biting, carrying with it a sense of isolation and solitude. Jagged peaks towered above, their icy crowns glistening in the pale sunlight. The mountains stood as ancient sentinels, weathered by time and scarred by the elements. The wind swept through narrow passes and whisted past spires of old rock jutting from the earth like the bones of Nephilim from some half-remembered tale told by abbey clergy.

"Back t'march!" came der Flechtemann's command. With a groan, the rebels stood and stretched, and fell back into the shambling gait that left their legs chafed raw.

Dieter noticed an odd look on Yakov's face as he watched Yakov fall back into step with Anna and him. Yakov appeared preoccupied with some notion he mulled over in his mind.

Anna noticed Yakov's absent focus as well. "What be the matter with ye?" she asked, her brow furrowed in question. "What has he been sayin' t'thee?"

Yakov looked at her, though she could not hold his glance for long. Looking absently away again Yakov answered curtly, "Naught that need concern ye."

"Yer a brother of mine, are ye not?" Anna argued. No response came back. Yakov continued to walk silently, as though lost in thought.

"This cause has work that needs doin'," he said finally, following a pensive pause. Unsure how Anna and Dieter would take his sincerity, he continued, "Ye asked if I believe—I do. And I believe, also, in what this cause be needin'."

"And what be that?" Dieter asked quietly, seeing the foreboding in Yakov's glance.

"Sacrifice," came the reply—and then, before Anna or Dieter could react, Yakov was striding up the line to der Flechtemann, prepared to put his plan in motion.

***

Mikkel's depressed feeling fit well with the overcast day. As a part of this whole affair, this sortie combing the hillside for several hours seeking some sign of the rebels met now with frustration. The hounds lost the scent of the partisans near a stream. A furious Chain then ordered his men scurrying to comb the hills for signs… any sign to determine in which direction the band moved. The trackers returned, now giving way to any success… the land too

73

rocky… the snow too loose… no track held for their pursuit-
-and so Mikkel found himself on a fool's errand.

With his ginger beard grown fuller and his hair rough and shaggy over the course of the march, Now a man in stature with intent and leadership, Mikkel stood as an imposing warrior. His aventail hung loose and clinked against his mail collar. In past combat splinters of a shattered arrow carved a map of scars along his neck, the longest of which drifted lazily onto his cheek, parting his red beard. Walking carefully, leading a search party through snarled brush and over sharp stubble, he suddenly sneezed, almost stumbling into a narrow crevice at the side of the treacherous pass through which a small group of scouts now searched. He gulped as one of the men beside him steadied him. Mikkel, looking to his rescuer… nodded in gratitude.

"Be a pox'd end to have died fer a sneeze," he chuckled sheepishly,… redfaced… embarrassed, Mikkel gathered himself. "Thank ye, Dumas."

The stoic mercenary nodded unsmilingly, returning to his duty. A mangy hound followed him, growling as it gave Mikkel a warning growl.

Mikkel sighed, the last thing he wanted was to work beside mercenaries again, much less the Chain's unwashed lot—yet here he was, marching south into a frozen hell at the Chain's beck and call. Though the life of a soldier suited him well, the past month took him to his limits. The chief perks of soldiering—alcohol, women, and loot—dwindled. Moving along now with his small clothes, those clothes worn closest to his skin, frozen stiff, he yearned for the warmth of the barracks in Schoningen. Ever since the ambush—

But, no, he didn't like to think of the ambush.

"Here!" came a call as the hounds began to bark.

74

"What have we?" Mikkel asked, hurrying as much as he could as he sequeezed through a narrow gap. He lowered his head as he passed under an outcrop, only to hear a man desperately pleading.

"Nay, I am not of them—believe me! I ran from tha' lot, oh Lord, oh please forgive me…"

That voice, Mikkel thought in wonder. *No, it couldna' be—could it?*

As the growling of the dog grew louder, Mikkel finally came upon the scene—Dumas and another soldier stood above a hunched, bleeding figure, as the war-hound growled and snarled. The figure, lanky and shuddering, looked up with large, hollow eyes, his face a bloody mask.

"M—Mikkel?" the man said in broken amazement.

"Lord be praised," Mikkel breathed. "Yakov?"

Chapter VI: False Face

-Brother Jakob, circa 1383

"Where is he?" Anna sputtered, nearly mindless with rage barely able to be restrained by Dieter, trying his best to pull her back from the rebel leader's throat.

Anna's breaths emerged in furious puffs, visible in the frigid air, her chest heaving with rage, concern, and heartache. Her wild, uncombed hair fluttered in the cold gusts of wind buffeting the mountains, framing her flushed face as she struggled against Dieter's firm hold.

Der Flechtemann stood before her, motionless. His finger twitched as he looked at her—and whatever he felt in that moment never made it to his face. Cold and hard, as ageless and immovable as the mountains around them, no trace of regret or sadness showed.

Around the spectacle, the rebels stood frozen in place. Their loyalty to their leader on one hand, on the other, they grew fonder of Anna—she represented to most, in some ways, the mother of the camp, always there with a kind word or help. As the father and daughter fought, observers reached the

76

same conclusion— staying away from taking any side in the argument may be the wisest path to tread.

"Yakov is servin' the cause," the rebel leader finally said in a slow, measured tone. Anna spat at the snow between them.

"Where did ye send him? Where did ye send mine brother?" she demanded as she displayed her agitation. "Has he nay suffered enough? Has he nay already lost too much? What kind of a rotten father are ye, to send yer own flesh—"

"Hold!" der Flechtemann interrupted raising a hand, palm towards Anna. "I sent him not," anger flashed in his eyes for the first time.

"Then…?"

"This be Yakov's plan—his vision," der Flechtemann responded, his voice now more restrained. "He came t'me himself."

The tension in the air crackled with unseen electricity. Dieter, resolute yet on the edge of restraint, echoed Anna's inquiry, his tone deliberate and firm.

"Where is our brother," Dieter asked, nearly incapable of restraining Anna's wrath.

"He has gone amongst the enemy," der Flechtemann said with simple explanation. "He has gone t'be our eyes and ears."

Anna's eyes bore into der Flechtemann, anguish and disbelief swirling in their depths. Her breathing rose and fell in a ragged rhythm, her gaze flickering between the rebel leader and the snowy ground, as Dieter's grip on her shoulders grew gentler. He shifted his weight in the snow,

77

uncertain about what all of this could mean. His breaths, too, emerged like little clouds of frost.

In the midst of this tension two scouts, one burly, one sinewy, appeared, their faces covered by tattered scarves to ward against the cold. They looked at the confrontation uneasily, as though wondering if to speak.

"What be thy report?" der Flechtemann asked of them, relieved by the distraction.

"We slew one o' theirs," the more burly scout reported, holding up a bright silver chainmail shirt and a new honed shortsword. "Feller saw our faces though." He looked at the other scout and gave an affirming shrug. "We took what be readily available. As for a path—"

"Yon passes afore us are manned 'n patrolled," the sinewy scout interjected, scratching at his overgrown hair. "Nay no layabouts neither, nay—tha' lot's bedecked in silver-bright mail, most carryin' spears, fine black shields, and daggers in sheaths at their side attached to baldricks hung shoulder to waist across their chest."

"There be old trails, hunting routes and so on, visible to them who's familiar with the mountains," the burly scout added quickly. "Old markers tied to the branches o' dead trees and the like, left there t'aid local folk durin' the storms. An' there be settlements up in the mountains as well— though seems right mad t'me t'live there."

Der Flechtemann nodded with satisfaction of the report. "I ken yer meanin' lads." Pointing to the equipment the two scouts brought back, he indicated. "Fer thy new provisions, share that mail with one of the cavalrymen, and keep the blade. Fer now, we shall nay take the pass then, but move swift up yon marked old paths, and put our lives in the common hands o' them what's left these signs." Addressing
78

the Sinewy scout directly, der Flechtemann asked, "Where did ye see the nearest such path... Point it out t'me."

"An hour t'the south, half-hidden by a dead tree."

Der Flechtemann nodded. "We make fer there."

As the line began to hesitantly move again, the cold creeping into their moist clothes, the group having stayed in one place too long. Der Flechtemann looked at Anna, who still stood frozen in place, angry eyes locked on her father. Dieter's arm around her seemed more supportive than anything else, too, the young man joined his sister in her visual accusation of his father with something akin to derision.

"Half a rebel and a headful o' guilt," Dieter said slowly. "That's what mine brother is—and ye know so. Ye could have forbidden him, had ye a heart fer anythin' but thy cause."

"Nay, I will repeat myself, so listen," der Flechtemann said, his eyes darkly determined. "The cause comes first—and yer brother knew this. His path chosen by him on his lonesome seeks only fer ye t'be safe—and for our cause t'succeed, no matter what it takes. He shall mislead the enemy and grant us a window into the minds of that ragged lot."

Anna's fury grew cold and lifeless, her gaze distant as she looked down at the snow. "And so he believed—but at what cost, my Yakov?" Her voice distant, tinted by a quiver, a hint of vulnerability creeping in.

The frigid air all but swallowed her words as it burst against the walls of the obscure path. The bitter cold seeped into their bones, and as her wet eyes burned against the cold, Anna wondered when she would see her brother again.

79

***

As the sun descended, its last rays cast a somber hue upon the skeletal remains of trees, long stripped of their foliage, loomed the dying light. Nestled among this desolate scene a mercenary camp, a gathering of tents and makeshift shelters, clung to a low incline, sheltered by the bent trees. Tethered near the outskirts, hounds whined. Their cries echoed mournfully against the stark mountainside as a solitary fire burned in the center of the camp, its flames a striking, almost blood-like red against the surrounding snow. It crackled and hissed, offering slight warmth against the encroaching night, its glow reflecting off the snow in an almost macabre dance.

Mercenaries and soldiers, clad in mail, patched gambesons, and worn cloaks, milled about the flame. Some sharpened blades, while a few sat huddled together, sharing terse conversations. As they spoke, their eyes flicked to the newcomer, their camaraderie, born more out of necessity than any true sense of kinship.

Yakov huddled close to the crimson flame; his bony shoulders covered by a shawl. His gaze fixed on the flickering flames, and even though he sat close the chill of the mountain air seemed to cut through the layers of his clothing—though perhaps it was just fear at the thought of the ruse he now found himself involved. The rebels, and his family, remained hidden somewhere within the same ominous peaks towering on each side of him. For this distraction to work it now became necessary for Yakov to fall back in with his old soldier friends who hunted his family. His frayed nerves shuddered amidst the chatter and clinking of armor around him, and his heart raced with every exchange, every jesting comment, each word, and movement scrutinized for any hint of his true allegiance.

80

Wha' if they ken me purpose? He wondered in dread. *Wha' if they know?*

He kept his gaze low, focusing on the fire's dance of light and shadows, concealing the turmoil within. The rebels' cause burned brighter in his heart than ever before—and yet, to preserve the cause, the deceit must be maintained. The image of Anna and Dieter flashed into his mind, and almost idly, he wondered if he'd see them again.

None of that, he scolded himself. *Y'found your way back once, Yakov, and y'will again.*

Just then, Mikkel sat next to him, offering him a strip of dried meat. Yakov took it gratefully, taking a tough, salty bite.

Sitting together, the two made an odd pair. They were similarly tall, yet months of being on the move living on foraged goods took its toll on Yakov. Always lanky, his falling weight created sunken features identifying eyes and cheeks. With his skin tight against the cheekbones, a prominence to his dark beard framed his face yielding to the gaunt countenance he now embraced. Unruly black hair fell on his forehead and scratched at the back of his neck. His feet were covered with split calluses. His ears smarted, red in the cold.

Grown into his knobby limbs, Mikkel now exhibited a more muscular body. The contrast Yakov viewed in Mikkel created a widely different picture than the one he remembered of the wide-eyed youth hiding behind a tree. Mikkel seemed self-assured now, much like a man who knows well his lot in life.

"By the saints, I thought ye were gone and burried," Mikkel finally said, before smiling lopsidedly. "But ye always were a crafty culprit."

81

"It is well to see ye too, Mikkel," Yakov chuckled, a sense of unease gnawing him beneath a facade of relief.

Sitting closer to the warmth of the fire, they shared uneasy tales of their former unit, recounting battles, and shared hardships. Yakov listened more than he spoke, his mind juggling the memories of his past life with the cloak of deceit he now wore. He wondered how long he could sustain this pretense. The risk to his person in the endeavor to create a distraction should it not succeed, could not only cost his life, but could potentially jeopardize the lives of those rebels he held dear.

As the fire crackled the sky deepened into the dark of night and stillness settled over the encampment. The chill of the mountain air deepened, and Yakov steeled himself to the task at hand. His loyalty now belonged entirely to the rebels. He pledged himself to this undertaking with his quiet oath to der Flechtemann. His intension to honor the commitment saw no bounds... no matter what that may mean.

There was a lull in their conversation as Mikkel poked at the flames with a stick. Eventually, he spoke.

"Where have ye been? We thought the rebels took thee. I s'pose, they did—but what...how...?" Mikkel trailed off, genuine concern yet supicious curiosity shadowed in deep, etched lines on his face.

Yakov's heart heavy with apprehension, hesitated with the weight of the back-story he now invented for his plan. "Aye, they did. Dragged me' round for many a foul month, through prickly bushes and foul waters. First, they made me show 'em the quiet ways 'round Schoningen. But after a time, I was naught but a servant to 'em. They did nay bind me—see, there are no marks on me wrists—but they jeered and dared me t'try. Claimed they needed t'practice

82

with their bows. Two o'the other prisoners tried t'run—they didn't make it more 'un twenty paces from camp."

"By all the saints," awed, Mikkel took a deep breath shaking his head in unbelief, then let it out. "How'd ye break free?"

Yakov shifted uncomfortably. "'Twas hard, Mikkel. They got used to me, thinkin' I couldn't escape this frozen, cursed place—knowin' I'd freeze if I tried to run, that I showed the sense to keep my will to do so low. But nay, 'twas better to die alone than as their slave. I waited for the right time to slip away. Nay found by yer mercenaries I would've sure frozen in the wild."

Mikkel's hand rested on Yakov's shoulder in a gesture of solidarity. "It's a right miracle y'made it. As I said, yer a crafty bugger. It's good t'see ye—and y'look better than I'da thought, seein' as what ye been through."

Yakov managed a weak smile, unsure of how to respond.

Mikkel's dower expression softened, sympathetic lines etched on his face reflected some of the comradery the two once shared. "Now, look—yer fine and safe now, aye? We're here for ye, Yakov, or at least I am. I missed yer sour face—march has been right dull without ye."

Yakov hesitating, proceeded cautiously. "But is it true, Mikkel? This band o' yours is led by…" He paused, bile rising in his throat. "…*him?*"

"Oh, 'tis true, aye," came a voice, and Yakov's spine froze. A familiar voice, unplaceable and singsong, raw and cruel, interrupted the conversation between the one-time friends. Beside him, Mikkel grew stiff as well.

Yakov turned to see a face he wished he could forget—a face that still swam in his dreams, like a boat in a sea of blood. A leathery, rugged face, with a prominent brow and an eternal grin, glared, with an amusing smirk, back at the two. Red hair, longer than he remembered, flared around a high forehead. A cruel, unsightly scar twisted the man's right cheek, the cheekbone visibly distorted by the wound; a remembrance Yakov knew well.

Petres the Chain laughed at the look on Yakov's face.

"Oh but I know ye," he said pleasantly. "Both o' ye are my findings, nay? I plucked ye from some village, or as likely, some wee town a mere gob's throw from bein' a village." The Chain paused. He continued with pointed accusation. "I plucked ye from the dirt and made men of thee."

Yakov remained fearfully quiet, his throat felt swollen, his mouth dry, while a dull ache thudded like a drum in his temple. Petres held his arm firmly, pulling him up. Yakov complied, like a marionette on stings at the will of the puppeteer, in shock at the strength in the man's broad arm.

"Up ye stand," the Chain said, through a hubris grin before looking around at the mercenaries who peered back in caution. "See here—such is the stock o' man as I make." Now turning Yakov for all to see. Petres continued, "He lives some months with poxed rebels as masters, an' he escapes without a scratch… amazing." Now sneering at Yakov, the Chain claimed scornfully, "What a breed of man, aye?... Say aye!" He challenged.

The mercenaries complied half-heartedly with a smattering of aye's, not looking up, all too aware of their leader's eccentricities. Mikkel studied the Chain tensely, his eyes flicking from him to Yakov. Around them, silhouettes of dead trees cast long, eerie shadows that stretched across the snow-covered ground.

Yakov went cold with eminent awareness of possible danger. *The Chain suspects. He knows, he has to know.* He worried.

"Hath been a while since I've known thee," Petres said, clapping Yakov conspiratorially on the back. "What say, then… ye and I acquaint ourselves, each t'the other?" Stopping, he faced Yakov gesturing between Yakov and himself, a false wonderment curling in the twist of one eyebrow. Then taking Yakov by the elbow proceeded to move aside. "Here, come with me. We shall walk."

"Then I shall come, too," Mikkel said, moving to stand from his seat on a log near the firepit.

"Ye shall not!" The Chain emphatically pronounced. Then looking into Mikkel's eyes, his demeanor changing ever so slightly, he continued, "so be not a fool," Petres cold utterance pronounced as a deadly dagger thrown true. "Sit yerself back down, man."

Mikkel paused, then sat down slowly, giving Yakov a helpless glance. Yakov nodded back, a short, pale nod. Now turning, Yakov followed the Chain as the latter turned. Above them, faint stars began to emerge one by one in the darkening sky, their distant twinkles providing the only relief from the oppressive darkness.

Yakov paced alongside Petres the Chain, the sadistic leader of the mercenary band given the task of suppressing the partisan revolt. A façade of composure, along with the weight of scrutiny by Petres, weighed on Yakov as he continued with his intended mime… his plan of deception.

85

They strolled through the dimly lit camp, the air thick with the smell of burning wood and damp earth.

"Yakov be yer name, aye?" Petres asked.

"Aye, sir. Yakov Symon."

"A strange name, fer a strange lad," Petres grinned wonderingly. "What were ye afore I found ye? An orphaned Pole, fleein' village t'village? Or were ye born of a witch, an ol' crone in some forrest?" The Chain quarried with cunning disguise in his now soothing voice.

Petres questions provoked ire in Yakov. "Nay, neither," He said, trying to hold back a flare of contempt. "I'm a man as any other—I grew on an homestead, not far from—"

"So, now, friend Yakov," Petres interrupted, his voice dripping with a disconcerting politeness. "Yer back in thine fold. Back amongst conscripts and bloody spears. An escape from our afear'd rebels, eh? Quite a tale ye have there." His tone casual, but his eyes, now fixed on his target, bore through Yakov, searching as he probed for any crack in the façade presented by the perplexity before him.

Yakov offered a tight-lipped smile, now cautiously beginning to feel gratification in the fact his ploy appeared to move toward his benefit. "Aye, sir. It weren't rightly easy by any chance, but I flew as I was able."

Petres's voice, gruff and chilling, emitted a soft, sly chuckle. "Ah, the tales a man hears sellswordin' are worth it all. Hired a time ago by a lord o'fame, a knight in the true sense, nay a mercenary as me, I knew a man. He be a regular man as ye, who said he'd seen Death ridin' abroad, black-hooded and skull-spurred. Y'know what I told 'im, friend Yakov?"

86

"That he drank too much?" Yakov said, a false smile still frozen on his face.

Petres laughed heartily, clapping Yakov's back again. "Oh, I like ye, lad. Me point bein', yer story is nay half as amusin', yet it be of interest." The mercenary knight paused as if to argue with himself over some thought in his mind…. Perplexed he continued, "Rebels! Slippery folk, ain't they? They gave me this, y'see."

Petres jabbed a thick finger at his scar, a grim look in his eye. Yakov nodded slowly.

"Was ye there at that battle?" Petres with a conspiratorial whisper, leaned in close.

"Nay, sir," Yakov stammered then quickly redirected his admission. "Or I was, but saw nothing'. I told tha' lot the trade routes, but aside from that, they left me with their rearguard."

"All me life," Petres quietly, but with treacherous intent, began to reason, a distant look clouding his gaze. "I thought me'self a rebel. Oh, aye, rebels come in all walks. The allegiance depending on who may pay the most. I found more worth in the coin of crownlings and fat old men. I killed fer their gain—but nay, not fer them… 'twas done fer me. A rebel I be… me against the world! But that day, friend Yakov, I learned t'hate the lot."

Yakov nodded slowly.

"Friend," the Chain suddenly, the interrogator's smile returning, "Tell me now, as easily as ye told the rebels. What did ye learn of them? What did ye learn as ye languished in their fine care?"

87

"Nay much, sir," Yakov said, maintaining his composure. He knew to keep the Chain offguard as long as possible would be the only way the rebels could increase the distance between the two groups. "They're a right secretive lot, tight-knit and the like. I was but a prisoner, not far privy to their plans..."

"Der Flechtemann," Petres mused. "Tha' name is what confounds me. It itches in me skull, just outside reach; His name mentioned in quiet reverie like a legend of old." The Chain showed more frustration while he continued, now ranting, "Now a story told by village-rats an' the like. What's this fellow like, then? Ye must have some inkling o'this cursed leader of theirs—I am a hunter, see, and I must know mine prey." He demanded, the pitch of his voice reaching angry high tones.

"I saw him, aye," Yakov nodded, drawing in a quick breath. "Though mostly from afar, sir… a figure in the shadows, feared and respected among his followers."

Petres's smile widened, calming again he, smiling a Cheshire grin, revealed a row of yellowing teeth. "Oh, fear'd and respected, ye say? Rightly mysterious, rightly powerful. Already, we have at least one man missing—perhaps he lies in a ditch with an arrow in his eye. No matter… but per'aps we should have a chat one of these days about our elusive der Flechtemann. Remember all ye can of him. I trust yer mind shall remember more in time, aye?"

"Aye, sir," Yakov said. "I'll… try… to remember."

"And remember this, also," Petres smiled warmly, putting a heavy hand on Yakov's shoulder. "Should ye betray my lot, I shall have thee flayed before me, and visit 'pon ye such misery as t'make the apostles weep. Does ye ken my meanin'?"

88

"Aye," Yakov said quietly, his mouth chalk dry.

"Fer now, friend Yakov," Petres continued, inclining his head meaningfully. "Mayhaps ye can enligh'en me regarding yon ruffian lot's current location?"

Slowly, Yakov nodded. Still speaking, they continued their uneasy stroll, the cold air thick with deception and dread. Yakov felt the deception slowly gaining ground.

Chapter VII: Bloodied Hand

"We tell the tales of holy wars, holy killings, holy executions—yet holy is only that which lives, say I...though all try to justify. Yet no water is holy, no well as deep, as to wash clean a bloodied hand..."

-Brother Jakob, circa 1382

A week passed.

Yakov struggled to balance the weight of his double life. As he sat among Mikkel and a few other men on stump stools or dirty blankets near a campfire, laughter rang hollow in his ears.

Mikkel, regaling the group with a bawdy joke, elicited raucous laughter from the men. Yakov's chuckle, more a facade than a genuine expression, joined in with the chorus, though his mind wandered. Tonight was the night.

As the laughter ebbed, Yakov feigned a casual tone. "Right, lads, I need t'take a leak." He stood.

With a nod from Mikkel and nonchalant acknowledgments from the others, Yakov slipped away from the circle, leaving the warmth of the fire behind.

He moved swiftly, staying to the flame's edge of the camp… his heart pounding in his chest. The memory of his conversation with der Flechtemann loomed over him. He knew a contact waited for him. Hiding briefly, he waited for one of the scouts to look away. Now he darted into the shroud of night that enveloped the mountainous terrain. His movements were deliberate and silent, treading the shadowy pathways while eluding the sharp gazes of the camp sentries. The cold air bit into his skin as he navigated the labyrinth of trees and rugged terrain, each step a calculated risk.

Two nights ago signal sparks in the distance, lit by a tinderbox identified where he was to meet his rebel contacts.

As he tentatively crawled through the rocks, he spotted a solitary figure from the darkness ahead, marked by the familiar, pockmarked face of Elias. Their eyes met in a silent acknowledgment.

Elias nodded. "Yer late," he murmured, his voice low.

"I had t'see folk didn't notice," Yakov whispered in response, his breath clouding in the crisp air.

Elias's looked at Yakov, his eyes inscrutable. "Well? What have ye learned?"

"Fer one, I've diverted the Chain's attention. I have sent him seekin' the wrong course, just as ye told me," Yakov whispered. "But in only a while, I have seen Petres seeks not the rebels—he seeks der Flechtemann. Though he is bein' paid t'eliminate the threat o' rebellion, this is but a game to 'im, a hunt fer my father.

Elias nodded grimly. "Aye, that matches what little I know of him. He shall not be content with a liver-shot, or an arrow to our eye—his steel seeks our heart, and that be thy father. Der Flechtemann's survival is the nape of our cause."

The strain of the ruse foraging for intelligence of the Chain's movements showed on Yakov's face. Too much quarry and discussion of logistics could only draw attention to the fact Yakov presented a new side to his allegiance. His tone softened as he changed the conversation to more need-to-know intentions. Yakov did not like the subterfuge drawing Mikkel, his former friend, into his plot, but then again his understanding of the issues surrounding the patriots cause now placed his friend squarely on the opposite side of a line drawn in the soil by all parties. And too, simply, his heart ached with longing for word of his family. Having given Elias the information necessary, Yakov asked, "Now ye tell me—how be they? My sister, my brother...be they safe? Well? Has ye found luck in foragin'? Tell me of the camp."

Elias's expression remained guarded. "They're well, safe, and nary yer worry. Keep thine eye on thy work, and yer mind on yer act."

Yakov sensed he would get nothing from the tight-lipped rebel, his pockmarked face cold in the dark. With an audible exhale, understanding the risk of delving further, he let the subject drop.

"How long have ye till yer missed?" Elias asked.

"I must be off," Yakov muttered, looking behind him. "Mikkel, even now, shall wonder at the breadth of me bladder fer takin' so long."

"Then look here," Elias said, handing him a parchment—Yakov unfurled it, but it was too dark to make much out. "Nay, ye shall not be able to see much now, but here etched be the letters of Latin, the tongue o' Christendom. I shall teach it thee, if only fer us to communicate better. Take this, and memorize these letter shapes. Next we meet, I shall teach thee more."

Yakov nodded hesitantly. "How do ye know such things?"

"Now is nay time fer questions," Elias muttered. "Fly from here, lest yon unwashed beasts of the Chain come huntin' for thee."

"Aye," Yakov nodded reluctantly. "Give me family a sign of good health fer me."

With that, they parted ways. The parchment hidden away in a pouch dangling from his loose belt, Yakov felt renewed, a sense of determination filled his bearing. The burden of the secrets he carried, still heavy, at least gave him something he could do—a way to atone for the horrors still haunting his dreams. The night swallowed his figure as he hurried back to the camp, his thoughts already drifting with eagerness. He'd learn the clandestine code of symbles making phrases of Latin. With this new skill Yakov knew passing on important messages to the rebels of the movement and strategy planned by the mercenaries would be invaluable.

Now returned to the mercenary encampment in the evening just after sundown, the array of sputtering campfires and low tent shelters rested their sleepy selves, signaled by snoring coming from some of the tents and covered lumps of shadows around warming fires. Too, a few stragglers crawled into the open maw of their tent portals to find comfort for the night ahead. Alone by a campfire Mikkel, with a raised eyebrow, watched Yakov approach "Here he is! What were ye off for, lad? I feared that ye lay in some bush with a rebel's arrow in yer throat."

93

"I see how worried ye be," Yakov laughed, feigning a convivial posture for his friend, his nerves still a little on edge from his ploy with Elias. "Ye have nay moved an inch from the flame, warm and content as ye be." He chided, then changing his mirth to more control, he continued, reassuring Mikkel, "But nay, I have drunk too well in too short a time."

"Then mayhaps I should name ye Yakov Ironbladder," Mikkel joked with a deep chuckle. Yakov grinned as well, though it didn't reach his eyes. A stone of worry still lay at the bottom of his stomach. Suddenly, he wanted to come clean—he wanted to tell Mikkel everything, about the rebels, about der Flechtemann, about the cause. He wanted—no, he *needed*—to let him know, to relieve the weight on his soul. Surely, Mikkel would understand. Surely, he would not betray him to the Chain.

Surely not.

"Mikkel, I—" Yakov began, then paused.

"Hm? What is it?" Mikkel asked, curious.

As he looked at his friend, Yakov suddenly realized how much like a soldier Mikkel looked. He remembered, then, how Mikkel lost his family, how conscription now gave him everything bandits took from him—camaraderie, power, and a place to belong. Suddenly, Yakov knew it could not be so simple a thing to trust Mikkel... *friend or no*, he thought.

"Nay, nothing," Yakov smiled weakly. "I have missed thee, that be all."

Mikkel laughed with jovial delight and punched him in the shoulder at which Yakov grimaced. "Has sufferin' turned ye soft, man?" Mikkel quipped. He continued reassuringly, "All is well though my friend, fer I have missed yer ugly face as well."

Their laughter continued as they sat by the fading fire, though Yakov's laughter rang hollow in his ears.

***

"Listen, t'me!" the Chain roared. Every soldier in the gathering turned their eyes upon him. "There be a village on the slopes, yonder." He pointed to the south. "—and already, they show us naught ken of the rebels' whereabouts. They hide their hand against us and speak of nothin' to our messengers. They avoid us and look down from the scree o' their fallin' palisades as though from the walls o' Hohensalzburg. But this be nay castle, and these be nay warriors."

An ugly cheer growled from the guttural response of the men, and Yakov felt cold. He felt the cold of an otherworldly experience as if floating above and looking down on himself from a distance, horrified at what lay before him.

Yakov wore a burnished kettle-helm, a footman's gambeson, a shirt of chainmail, and a single spare gauntlet worn protecting his right hand and forearm. In his hand he also grasped a heavy glaive thrust into his care by the Chain himself. The glaive, its weight, now uncomfortably nestled against the curve of his shoulder, did not carry as much of the awkward realization the false directions given to the Chain which now, unexpectedly, brought the mercenary band to this small village nestled against sheer cliffs. A single path led up the slope toward thatched, snow-choked roofs peering over ledges protected only by a flimsy palisade of half-cut logs. *More likely this structure served more to protect the livestock from plummeting to their death than*

95

holding back a company of bloodthirsty mercenaries, Yakov surmised.

"Our provisions be runnin' low as well," Petres declared, his eyes shining as if already envisioning acts of violence. "We'll take as we can, and ye'll have what ye desire—women, wine, and plunder. And yet, ye must leave survivors. I have a specific goal fer taking that village— finding the whereabouts of der Flechtemann and his rebellious group. This be the final stop before the mountain passes—if that blackguard hath passed here unseen, he be already too far t'chase. But I believe it not! He be close, and we shall have him. Now form ranks! Form ranks, ye hounds o'death , and may I see thee hotblooded and strong on the other side!"

A bustle erupted from the band of men as the Chain's lieutenants quickly formed the company into ranks. Yakov, standing beside Mikkel, his hands clammy, his face sallow, absently acknowledged a dull pressure as his friend clapped him on one shoulder. While doing so Mikkel adjusted the long pike he, himself carried.

"All shall be well this time," Mikkel said reassuringly, responding to Yakov's aloof attitude. "Nay an ambush by rebels this time—see, it just be some villagers, naught much else. Ye shall be fine."

Yakov looked at him uncomprehendingly.

Have ye forgotten so much? Yakov thought in surreal amazement. *Was thy village, too, nay just as this? Were thy people nay slaughtered? And now ye will be the slaughterer, the harbinger o' death—do ye not realize? Do ye nay ken the stench o' blood to be on thine own hands?*

96

But if any such realization actualized, it was locked in a box, deep within Mikkel's mind. In his friend's eyes, Yakov saw only a job that needed doing… just another day.

And I was the same, Yakov realized with a lurch.

A great dread growing in the pit of his stomach, Yakov left his position, and walked briskly up to the Chain. He could hear Mikkel hiss in caution behind him, but he could hear nothing but the blood rushing to his head.

The mercenary captain barked further orders as he saw Yakov approach from the corner of his vision.

"Sir," Yakov said, advancing toward Petres. "I have something to ask of ye."

"Hm?" the Chain raised a quarried eyebrow.

"Leave these folk be, sir," Yakov pleaded. "Or, at least, be lenient with them. Send me one time to parley, perhaps. One last warning—they be but innocents. Even if they protected der Flechtemann in defense, maybe of their own lives, their welcome would be out of hospitality. Nay punish them, naught."

The Chain's smile, thin and foreboding, slapped each of his large hands onto Yakov's shoulders. Now looking strangely through, Petres' distant eyes appeared to gaze at something beyond Yakov. "I," the Chain began then refocused his eyes on Yakov. "admire thine spirit, friend Yakov. I admire yer purity. Ye be a brave little mongrel to come to me, pleadin' fer nobodies, fer the chafe o' the world." He paused. "But such be nay how wars be fought—nor be it how subjects learn to obey." The Chain dropped his hands and turned to look once again in the direction of the village. "Already, they have shown their disrespect of our hunt— these be mountain men, proud and dismal, and they shall nay

97

ken unless *we* help them." Now turning back to face Yakov, he continued with determination in his countenance. "So nay, ye shall parley naught—nay, until they be shown the rod."

Yakov nodded slowly, his face pallid, blood now rushing, draining away to a heart already working hard with growing anger and anguish. The Chain chuckled, pushing him back into line. "There ye go now! Form lines! Prepare!"

Yakov felt himself once more beside Mikkel, who gave him an incredulous look.

"Yer lucky he didn't have ye whipped," Mikkel whispered. "What were y'thinkin', man?"

"I know not," Yakov muttered incoherently.

Then came the Chain's command. Yakov looked up to see the man, Petres the Chain, standing on a bolder beside the trail and moving an extended arm, his flat hand requiring the column to move forward towards the goal.

"Advance, men! Advance, and take what ye will!"

In step with the line, Yakov and Mikkel trudged up the mountainous terrain, the weight of their weapons seeming to double as they approached the outskirts of the village. It was daybreak, and the cold air was heavy, laced with dread. The quietude, at first, broken only by the rustle of dying leaves and the clank of armor and chainmail.

Then the silence shattered by a thousand shards of sound… a cacophony of elation and anguish as the mercenaries advanced and encountered the villagefolk.

To greet the mercenaries, mournful horns blew in the distance, signaling the presence of the ill-prepared militia who guarded the village. Yakov's heart raced in his chest, nausea and dread churning within him. He gripped his glaive tight, the cold, leather-wrapped wooden haft offering little comfort. The faint light of dawn glinted against Mikkel and the others, their faces hidden under their helmets.

Drawing closer to the village, distant shouts could be heard as well as the ringing clash of metal against metal. Now within bowshot, Yakov flinched as arrows flew past the army of soldiers, but these were not the black-tufted, well-aimed arrows of the rebels. They were brittle and flew in lazy arcs, clearly shot from ill-strung, unpracticed bows. Still, curses arose behind him as some of the men were struck. Yakov held his breath dreading the engagement before them.

In the initial rank, while a trained shield wall held, armed men hacked at the untrained village militia with axes and short, brutish swords, Yakov and Mikkel found themselves placed in the second rank. With long polearms and longer swords, they poked and jabbed blindly at the bunched-up militia beyond. The second rank did not have to work face to face with the enemy, for the fact, they could not see the enemy, so battle by feel became more the rule. Yakov, eventually, caught only glances of the men dying to protect their village. Head after head of dark hair fell, and panicked eyes seemed to shout through the gaps between writhing, stabbing, dying bodies.

Soon, mercenaries were spilling into the village as they burst through the palisade. The humble village looked miserable, though not half so as the sight of the ill-equipped militia, now struggling to retreat, wielding a motley array of rusty arms.

Mikkel's voice, barely audible above the din, shouted to his friend, "Stay by me, Yakov! Remember—cut as ye will, but leave survivors!"

99

Yakov nodded dimly, his heart heavy as the clash of combat continued around them. With each thrust, his glaive felt the give of flesh and bone. He fought, not with ferocity, but with a sense of desolation, trying to disable rather than to kill. Around him, the conflict still raged. The acrid scent of sweat and fear mingled with the metallic tang of blood. Over the din, Yakov could hear a panicked birdsong in the distance as the mountain birds awakened to the din.

The battle was short and brutal. Assuming the blame, Yakov found it difficult to look at the carnage all around. He gave the directions given to him by Elias to the Chain as a misdirection to save his family. In doing so, no information gave indication the route would be to this village. The cost to the villagers for the lives of his family and new friends now added even more weight to an already heavy sadness.

Soon, the militia's resistance came to a bloody close. As men surrendered, the sound of combat waned, replaced by the heavy silence of the aftermath, broken only by the soft moans of the wounded and the sniffling laments of the broken.

The dawn attack now accented by the sun's rise on the bloody snow, Yakov surveyed the scene. The once-idyllic village lay in disarray, its inhabitants, both innocent and those who once resisted, now dragged, the dead and the living. into the open. Screams could be heard as Mercenaries, already laughing and tearing into the houses for what they garnered as the rewards of war, confiscated, abused, and raped their way through the houses and homes of the once docile village.

The plan devised to allow the partisans to escape was not intended to carry these ramifications. The weight of his actions to secretly develop the plan now settled upon Yakov—here it was, yet another burden to carry. There was

100

never an intention of drawing harm to a third party, but by the cunning of Petres, harm came to this village. Yakov did not intend for this, but it came and he must carry blame all the same. He now became acutely aware, if not before, of the depths of the Chain's corrupt desire.

As the day passed, Yakov remained distant. His friend, Mikkel, clearly wanted to join in the looting, he could tell, but remained with him instead. For his part, the Chain continued to question the villagers and the elders—but no favorable information was cleaned by the rebels, as Yakov expected. In time, orders came from the leaders to gather the supplies and return to camp---the village would serve as their shelter for a time.

As the day wore on, Yakov and Mikkel and other mercenaries spent time trudging back and forth between the supply camp and the village, ferrying materials and goods. Finally, with night approaching and supplies moved, the two comrades made a campfire in a hollow at the edge of the village. They sat on either side of the warm blaze gazing tiredly into the approaching darkness.

As they sat, a hand fell on each of their shoulders. Both turned and quickly noticed the hand that held them, still blood stained from the events of the day. They froze as the Chain squatted behind yet somewhat between them near the backside of the campfire, his bloody hands clasping them with a claw-like grip. Yakov glanced up now looking into Petres' face, and for once, the mercenary was not smiling. For the moment the knight leaned ahead, staring into the fire.

"Ye mourn the innocent, don't ye, Yakov?" he asked in his low gravelly voice, looking back to the clandestine soldier.

"I do," Yakov said, and Petres nodded distantly, a weathered look in his eyes.

"'Tis a rare thing in our times. I knew an innocent soul once, aye," Petres began, his voice distant and dark. "Oh, a beauteous soul, so bright—"the mercenary paused in reflection. He continued. "He shinned like the youthful Christ, even to me own rotten eye. Fer y'see, he be my child, me boy. His light radiated for me. He trusted my judgement. Me pride could nay have shown more. The day I lost him—" the Chain paused in deep silence, then continued with a grind of his teeth masking his tone, a low growl now began deep within, becoming more even as it rose to the surface. "---that blackened day, I understood."

Yakov and Mikkel listened in breathless silence, dreading this glimpse into the Chain's depths.

"I understood light matters little," Petres continued, his voice returning to a whisper. "Good matters little. Innocence is t'be lost. All that matters to a man on this filthy patch of ground is respect… power and respect. I lost me son fer I be powerless—I know better now." The Chain paused, his anger gathering as if to explode. "But that dog der Flechtemann, his cunning hath *unmanned* me. In maiming me... a laughingstock I be. Me, *the Chain!*" he roared suddenly, spittle flying from his mouth. In the distance, taken aback by the outburst, the mercenaries busied themselves in work, dreading their captain's furor.

"Naught matters, friends," Petres said, staring again into nothing. "Naught matters but the stories we leave…and I fear me story shall not end with avenging myself."

"Why?" Yakov asked tentatively, venturing into what could be dangerous territory. He needed the information, but pushing too hard may make Petres

102

suspicious and destroy any attempt to gather intelligence for his father, Hans. He continued. "Had the villagers naught to say of der Flechtemann?"

"Damn the dog," Petres hissed, muttering incoherently to himself. Looking out into the dark of night, he continued reasoning with himself, "He hath flown through the passes somehow, I'm convinced—he should make roost in Toscana, perhaps, or take up sellswordin' himself. But I shall not freeze fer his rotten hide." Pausing abruptly and turning to Yakov, Mikkel and others gathered nearby, he commanded, "We head northwest in two days, yes two days. We shall make for the Banate of Bosnia. Connections reside there, aye. Pacts we can trust. I know the Pavlović. We lick our wounds and rest awhile…aye, some rest, some women…and all shall be well enough…"

Mikkel cleared his throat, and it was as if Petres snapped back to reality. Plastering another grin on his face, he clapped Yakov and Mikkel's shoulders once again. "Get ye both some sleep." Then acknowledging the field of soldiers as if nothing of significance happened, speaking to them, "All o'ye, rest now," he ordered. "Ye fought well! I have made good men of ye."

So, saying, he left. Mikkel and Yakov simply looked at each other in consternation, unsure of what to say. Yakov then looking at the bloody hand print left on his shoulder, could not help himself but touch it. *Is this the beginning of an insanity,* he thought.

***

The next night after the strange encounter with Petres, Yakov chose to once more steal away from camp to meet with Elias. The mercenaries were to leave the next morning and some urgency filled Yakov's mind. Gaunt and haunted, he crawled up a narrow path, using cold fingers to feel groves of Latin letters scratched into stones along the way and leading him forward. In time, a hooded figure appeared.

"Have ye memorized the letters?" Elias asked without preamble.

Yakov stared at him without emotion. "Y'knew there be a village here. Ye gave me these directions. Ye told me to send the Chain here. Y'sacrificed those lives."

Elias was quiet. The two simply weighed the tension trying to discern a next move or comment. Then, Elias walked forward until the two could see clearly the face of the other. Yakov looked into his contact's eyes, searching for regret. None could be found.

"I did what I must," Elias said, his voice betraying no emotion. "Having found no trace of der Flechtemann here, the Chain shall lose hope. He will dread he is too late, fer he has wasted a day on nothing. We be given time t'flee, t'regroup, to catch our breath. Yer brother sleeps tonight only because of mine actions—actions that ye condemn."

"Those actions have led to the death o'innocents," Yakov growled. "Does der Flechtemann know? My father would not do what ye determined."

"I have *protected* der Flechtemann—not to mention yer sister, and yer brother," Elias said, staring at Yakov darkly. "It matters not what der Flechtemann knows of it— but ye should know that if yer family survives this ordeal, it shall be for the decision *I* made. I do what I must fer this cause, the same as ye."

Yakov stood speechless in the dim darkness of night. His memories of the fight flooded back to him. After all,

104

militiamen lay dead because of his hand, too. He began to weigh events, his mind now realizing at least a part of the responsibility lay on him and the plan he thought to be carefully devised. What right had he to judge Elias? And though his helpless fury still bubbled, he knew nothing could now be done.

"The Chain believes der Flechtemann has escaped," Yakov finally said hoarsely. "We are to make fer the Banate of Bosnia."

Elias nodded, satisfied. "Good—then it is as planned. Have ye learned yer letters?"

"Aye, but…" Yakov looked at Elias squarely but with some hesitation. "Can't I return, now? The rebel's trail be lost to 'im. I can just return, and—"

Elias shook his head. "He shall be suspicious if ye disappear now. Y'must stay. I shall report what ye said here to der Flechtemann, and he shall plan what will be next. Fer now, look here—I shall teach ye some words."

Tired and defeated, Yakov looked quietly as Elias scratched words in the dirt, lit only by the waning moonlight. As he looked down, struck by a realization, perhaps a trick of the light, he decried his own hands which appeared to be covered in blood.

105

Chapter VIII: Lion's Pride

"What beast is as strong or noble as the lion? None that I know. It is great and it is beautiful. Yet the lion is unmade only for one flaw—it is too proud of being what it is, too strong to hesitate, and too noble to know better."

-Brother Jakob, circa 1383

The man opened his eyes and froze as he saw a face only inches from his. Rough and rugged, grey-bearded and weary-eyed, with shoddy cropped hair pulled back over a high, time-worn forehead, and green, ageless eyes looked at him with all the softness of stone.

"It is good that ye have awakened," der Flechtemann said, his voice dark and low. The prisoner looked at his surroundings only to see that he sat bound to a dying tree. Split at the top, perhaps by lightning, this tree revealed an ugliness to the setting. The captives breath fogged as he coughed. The air thin and frigid, swirled as a single snowflake touched his cheek. Its wet presence signaling more to come. Behind the face dominating his vision, the rugged, cold mountains loomed ominously, shrouded in mist.

"Ye were huntin' us, were ye not?" Der Flechtemann paused expecting a response then chuckled, "Ye came under the Chain's wretched command, scoured the stones with yer hounds—and yet, here ye be, taken by the very quarry ye seek," der Flechtemann said, now unsmiling. "Tell me, lad. What's yer name?"

The young mercenary shuddered. "Tilmann, sir. Please, I know nothin'…I saw nothin'. Jus' let me go, and I'll breathe nay a word, sir. I swear on me mother an' mine kin…" Breaking off, the young man gulped audibly as der Flechtemann pressed the blade of a knife to the hireling's throat.

"Speak only as asked," der Flechtemann frowned, pressing the dagger a bit firmer. "Why were ye combin' the region here…if the Chain's meanin' be t'leave?"

"I…how does ye…" the man sputtered, then gulped a second time as the cold metal of the held blade lightly caressed his neck. Pushing his back against the tree, becoming one with the tree as much as possible, trying to evade the intentions of der Flechtemann, he blurted, "I, we thought…we thought if we were t'find somethin' of ye, the Captain would have a reward…please…"

"And so ye has found us," der Flechtemann said smiling sardonically, then stabbing the knife into the bark of the tree above the lad's head. "That be nay hard, be it." The mercenary moved his head in affirmation while letting out a sigh of relief. "Now, ye shall tell me all I need to know. True?" Der Flechtemann looked with serious intent into the hireling's eyes.

"I…I know nothin' of what ye seek, I swear," Tilmann whined, rivulets of sweat dripping into his pale blue eyes. The perspiration from his brow smarted his eyes, and he squinted trying to force the sweat away. Suddenly, his eyes opened wide. In his restraint against the tree, he urgently struggled to peer around the rebels standing before him. "Where…where be the rest? Winfrid…?"

"Only ye survived our ambush," der Flechtemann said with little emotion.

107

"He be kin t'me," Tilmann said, his eyes wet.

Sighing, der Flechtemann stood up, then looking to his left he spied Elias. Tilmann followed his line of sight to a pockmarked man standing nearby, cold-eyed. "See he tells ye everything he knows," der Flechtemann instructed, pointing to their prisoner. "Then go seek me son. He'll have left ye a trail."

Elias nodded.

"Nay, please," Tilmann said, terrified of his demise. "Should I nay return? Guards'll ask where our party be." Trying to free himself from his bindings, he pleaded with reason as the rebels stirred to move. With a last effort the captive bellowed, "They shall know by our failure to return that ye be here."

"The mountains are treacherous," Elias said, retrieving der Flechtemann's knife. The young mercenary flinched as Elias grasped the knife and jerked it out of its embrace with the tree. Now speaking to the captive, he warned, "Speak well and free, and we shall see that ye live."

Der Flechtemann left the assembly. A few moments later he heared a muffled scream and then nothing. His heart clenched in his chest. The necessities of his rebellion weighted heavy, and the necessity of employing men like Elias always sat ill with him.

"So, this is what ye be," came a voice. Der Flechtemann turned to see his younger son leaning against a tree. Dieter, now a young man, seemed more gaunt than Hans last remembered—but then foraging on this accursed mountainside for untold days now reduced all to mere shadows of themselves. Dieter's once innocent eyes, now appeared as dark sockets, sunken from lack of rest to set his face in a perpetually grim expression.

108

"What does ye mean?" der Flechtemann said shortly.

"I mean that fer all yer talk o' goodness and decency," Dieter said, "Ye allow a man such as that t'inflict pain on another. Ye allow yer own son to sit coiled in a den o' vipers. Ye sacrifice virtue after virtue, yet ye ken yerself t'be a virtuous man, a good man, a leader fit t'follow."

"Nay," der Flechtemann said with quiet resolve. "I say nay such a thing, and I know m'self t'be much worse than ye can ken. And as fer yer elder brother, by his own device he be helping mislead our enemy—." Hans paused as he focused on Dieter, "I shall have him back ere he be discovered… On this, take me word."

"And why are ye ambushing their lot?" Perplexed, Dieter frowned. "Ye shall have them again on our heads."

Der Flechtemann looked at him evenly, one eyebrow raised. "I know the business o' struggle, lad. I've known it fer longer 'an ye lived."

With this, the rebel leader left, his back half-bent with an unseen weight. Dieter stood alone in the snow, hearing the muted mewls coming from the edge of camp. Despite his accusations, he knew der Flechtemann worried for Yakov. Everyone noticed it—since Yakov left, Hans grew even more withdrawn, seemingly more cautious, more careful in his plans. Yet Dieter knew the opposite true of his father. Even though his plans appeared cautious, to make no plans provided more opportunity to adjust. Too, in Dieter's mind, laying low and allowing the mercenaries to leave before making any firm decisions may be the safest answer.

Somehow, though, Dieter doubted disengagement with the Chain was anywhere near der Flechtemann's mind. He was to accustomed to their struggle, and to used to the inevitable fight.

109

With an unintended start, Dieter reacted with distorted ease as Elias emerged from the trees wiping the knife, taken from the tree above their prisoner's head, clean. Mulling over what his father said as well as the morbid demise of the prisoner, he gave Elias a nod in sober acknowledgement as he passed. Dieter understood the need for the squelching of corproal problems. Similar situations occurred in the past, but nonetheless, the cruelity did not feel right.

"I will see yer brother now," Elias said, noting Dieter's uncomfortable reaction to his appearance. "Have ye anything needin' to be said t'him?"

"Say I be in prayer fer him," Dieter said with quiet resignation.

Elias smiled, a rarity for the stoic man who knew an important lesson of survival now passed between the youngest of the siblings and himself. "With verses, or with thine heart?" He quarried.

"In my heart," Dieter muttered with an undertone of reluctance.

Elias nodded. "If ye wish fer verse, come to me on the morrow. I still have with me mine father's Bible. I shall read it for thee."

Dieter nodded noncomittaly, and the pockmarked rebel moved past, whispering something to himself. As he walked away, Dieter found himself shaking his head. The longer he stayed amongst them, the less sense the rebels made to him—a leader too proud to lay low, a godly torturer, and a son willing to put himself in the beast's belly for a cause he only half believed.

"There must be a better way," Dieter muttered in agitation as he walked back, trying not to hear the muffled whimpering at the edge of camp.

***

Another night now lay upon the encampment, and Yakov was early for once. The Chain recently saw fit to entrust him with sentry duty. In his assigned station, Yakov stood shivering at the post with naught but a faint flame for company. He wrapped a thick, quilted rag of a coif around his head under his kettle-helm to protect his ears from the cold.

Moving beyond the foot of the mountain, winter grew noticeably crueler. Blankets of snow lay over the trees and stone, and the rim of Yakov's helmet continued to grow heavier with the accumulation until periodically he shook the snow loose. Waiting patiently, He signaled Elias appropriately this time, covertly if clumsily, using a torch, for the past week, attempted leaving signs in Latin so the scout could trace their camp. Not always successful, he hoped Elias found his lettered trail for a meeting.

As Yakov scanned the perimeter, a click nearby alerted him. His hand instinctively gripped the haft of his glaive before relaxing as a silhouette moved among the shadows, standing at the very edge of the faint torchlight. Yakov took a step towards him, seeing the glint in Elias' eye.

"Yer here," Yakov said, relieved. "I wonder'd if ye'd followed my trail well. Was me Latin...?"

"Passable," Elias said in a low whisper somewhat perturbed by the diversion. "Though ye shall be no monk at this rate. No matter, thy skill, faint though it be, shall suffice in the comin' weeks. What news?"

111

"The Chain has grown strangely talkative, taking his loss hard," Yakov confided, his voice barely audible in the stillness. "He eats little but bread n' water, and he is mutterin' to himself each time I pass him. Near as I can piece, his march toward Bosnia is directed at some castle, only he be callin' it the *Toranj*. They're aimin' fer supply runs along the way. He has too many mouths t'survive on foragin'."

Elias absorbed the news, his brow furrowing in contemplation. Pale eyes flitted in the darkness. "Ye have done better than I expected, Yakov. I shall relay these smatterings to thy father."

"Tell 'im t'be cautious," Yakov blurted, then suddenly pulling his head down and whispering, noting the nervous cringe in Elias' eyes. "There be nothin' wrong I can sniff, but there be an…air o' wrongness 'bout the Chain's person. Somethin' be awry, I feel so. Tell 'im t'be cautious, t'rest his bow arm. Ye need to regroup, lay low, rest well…"

Elias looked questioningly at Yakov with sardonic amusement displaying an arch of one brow and an upturned curl at the edge of one end of his mouth. "Ye be yer father"s son in some ways, but in most ye are but a frenzied pup. Der Flechtemann shall nay sit idly by while ye march willynilly north. Rest fer us cannot come while the enemy grows strong. A message needs be sent to your father. Nay, it be not his nature to lie low; for, thy father be a lion, and like one shall he strike, as likely t'slay Petres as t'seize any spoils he secures."

Urgency crept cautiously into Yakov's tone as a nervous quiver, his worry evident. "Ye does nay understand, Elias. I fear this be a trap o' some kind. What if…what if he be retreatin' on purpose, only so ye may follow? He be a hunter, Elias, and if mine father be a lion, what better way t'bait such a beast than to look as prey? Ye must speak in his

112

ear. Ye must sing a song o' caution, tell him to stop his attack. It shall nay end well. For certain, I feel it in mine bones."

"Be calm… Ye know not yer clever father, I ken," Elias said. "But, he be ney prey fer some cunning device set by one who, being blinded by his own fury, does nay know the local inhabitants or discovered the lay o' the land. He shall not fall into no trap. The Chain knows naught what he trifles with, fer he stands nary a chance against der Flechtemann. I've served many men before, and naught, nay one says I, has thine father's mind. Ye must trust in yer father's direction lad. He will not let thee down, nor us, but ye must follow the plan as laid."

"And I have served with both," Yakov countered, hissing in frustration. "Me father be wise, aye, but in cunning, Petres has few equals. Do not presume tha' because we have won so far, that he be grown toothless. *Hear me, Elias*—I know thine loyalty to father be beyond reproach, but heed me. Warn der Flechtemann."

Elias shook his head, steadfast in his resolve. "I be tellin' ye, there be no haltin' him, and only a daft soul would dare. What he be wantin' ain't no gloom-spewin' pessimist—it be a band of ready warriors. What he be needin' be me fealty, me bow-ready limb, and me very breath if it comes to that, and so I pledge to him. He'll be stayin' a stride ahead, and ere long, our purpose will flourish. This be his stratagem, and we, the humble crew, knows how to dance to his tune."

Yakov felt a palpable sense of helplessness settling upon him. "Ye know not of what I speak."

Elias put a hand on his shoulder with with an air of certainty. "Hold faith, brother, and thine father shall deliver. Now I must away—continue t'leave signs, so we may pursue at leisure. Now a word to you, before I leave, know yer brother prays fer thee…" He paused in turning to leave. Elias looked back over his shoulder at Yakov for whom he garnered some fresh respect. "I shall, too."

With that, Elias turned and disappeared into the dark, his cloak blowing in the biting wind. A foreboding sense of helplessness carrying the uncertainty of the night, settled within Yakov as a chill breeze swept through the mercenary camp hidden on the other side of the brush behind him. Returning to the circle of the fire the flame flickered, and hurriedly he threw another scrawny branch into the embers. Sighing, he sat down on a stump, rubbing his gloved hands. Frustration, fear, and anxiety churned within him. His father, truly hell-bent on continuing his hunt of the Chain, as Elias seemed to imply, would be a mistake.

Contrary to what Elias said, Yakov knew naysayers were entirely what der Flechtemann needed. He needed voices of reason—but with Yakov's absence, Nerijus's naivety, and Sieghart being left in charge of the scouts foraging supplies all day, Elias' role in camp had grown. Now, no anchor held reason to der Flechtemann's genius—only an unquestioning follower, loyal to the point of fanaticism. His blind faith in der Flechtemann was no short of a zealot's faith in the church, and though Yakov knew his father understood all this at some level, a man like Elias was simply too useful and convenient to not make use of. As a consequence, now, there would be no stopping the lion.

Yakov's musings collapsed as he heard someone approach. With a clanking gait and the shuffle of snow, Mikkel's form clammered into view, rubbing his hands. "What news?" he called in a low voice, looking about.

"Naught but a quiet watch," Yakov said, noticing the way Mikkel was looking around. "Somethin' be afoot?" he asked breathing in deeply with concern.

"Odd, that," Mikkel grumbled fingering his beard. "Thought I glimpsed a… somethin' stir in the trees over there. But never mind, I reckon, fer I'm still half in dreams, half cozied in warmth, he recounted coming near the watchfire. Then suddenly, aware of the post, he asked, "Yet, Yakov, has nay a soul come to relieve yer watch? 'Tis the darkest part of the night. The other lad ought to be here by now"

"Nay, but all be well," Yakov smiled weakly, now breathing more easily. "I sleep little in any case."

Mikkel nodded thoughtfully. "Aye, I remember. Ye were never good at restin'. That mind o' yers never stops, does it?"

Yakov shrugged as Mikkel sat next to him with a sigh. For a few moments a quiet pause thickened the air between the two, and then Mikkel spoke.

"Y'know ye can tell me anythin', right?"

"I know," Yakov replied, the weight of guilt heavy in him. He also knew Mikkel could not possibly know the extent of the memories haunting him.

"Good," But subconsciously Mikkel, concerned with the grim wear of time appearing around Yakov's eyes, and at the lines of worry etched deep into his friends face, hesitated. "I'm no good a' this, but should ye need a stout drink and a good talk, be nay too proud t'come t'me. Aye?"

115

"Aye," Yakov said, smiling, his anxieties held at bay momentarily. The night passed quietly without further event.

Chapter IX: Sleeping Devil

"...And within us each is a sleeping devil. We call it something [other] than us, and pray it never wakes. We blame and curse it...not knowing that it is only us—for inside, it is you and I—and if we had but wisdom, we would let sleeping devils lie..."

-Brother Jakob, circa 1382

The horse in a slow canter, Elias astride the saddle said a quick prayer. Many payers passed his lips during these past days. Most of the prayers brought forward the cause— and though der Flechtemann would not participate, Elias prayed for his leader's soul as well.

As far as Elias was concerned, the only godly man in this entire empire, was the man he now served. He was closer, certainly, to the spirit of the old testament than any of the pompous old churchmen Elias encountered. As he rode, mindlessly swaying in the saddle with the gate of the horse. Within the fog of near sleep, the partisan reminisced about his father, a fat, balding priest with watery eyes, arriving to their cottage once a year, every year, to check on his illegitimate family—a family he should never have conceived. Elias huffed a heavy breath from deep within his chest, as did his horse echoing Elias' sentiment.

Now, as he rode along, a worm of worry crept into his mind. For several weeks now the rebel column used stealth and cunning to enjoy a more offensive posture to trail the mercenaries back towards the north. Elias placed trust in two of the best trackers in the partisan party keen to the ways

117

of spy craft to follow the trail left behind by Yakov. Snow made tracks and clues more difficult to find, even an army's, for trails did not last long in the wintery bluster, in which the going became slow and unpredictable. Yakov's carvings made the stalk easier, which allowed the scouts the ability to follow without getting uncomfortably close to the mercenaries. With his trail of broken Latin to follow, Yakov identified the way forward.

And then, two days ago, the trail disappeared altogether.

No report came on that day. Usually, every three days, one of the scouts would ride back and apprise der Flechtemann of the enemy's movements, but no word made its appearance this time. Now, his scouts ahead of the rebels, he rode with two other men of his section to accompany him, Elias became concerned with what may have happened to Yakov.

The answer did not elude him for long. With the sound of a bee passing close to his ear, out of the corner of one eye, Elias spied an arrow catch one of his men in a shoulder.

"Ambush!" Elias yelled, alarmed, the trio of rebels immediately scattered as more arrows flew. Over an incline, protected behind a drift of snow, were half a dozen mercenaries, armed with bows and arrows. Faint voices caught Elias' ear.

"I got 'im! Got 'un!" Came a shout from the slope.

"Keep shootin' ye fool!"

Incompetant, Elias thought, whistling a signal to his men as he drew his bow. Immediately, the rebels began to ride in a lazy circle around the incline as the confused archers

118

missed shot after confused shot into the snow. Drawing back an arrow on his stout recurve bow, Elias took aim, and let loose. Instantly, one of the mercs sprouted a feathered flower fed by a river of blood from his throat. The man fell forward with a gurgling lurch. Panicked, the other mercaneries began to fire with even poorer aim—one by one, the rebels with the advantage of movement on horseback, scored hits quickly. The ambush intended by the mercenaries to be a surprise, met their quick demise by the reaction of rebels used to strike and run tactics. No mercenaries survived the brief melee.

A casualty of the brief encounter, however, found an arrow buried in the neck of Elias' horse, who reared up, a crimson streak jetting over Elias' thigh. Wide eyed, Elias leapt from the saddle into the snow, rolling as he hastily tried to take aim as another arrow buried itself in the snow next to him. His horse, still rolling in the snow, nearly rolled over him before he could scramble to a safe distance. With that, arrows stuck the last two mercenaries, who fell in a crimson and white pool, of blood and snow mixed with that of the horse. His men rounded back towards Elias, one of them pale-faced and bleeding. They now watched quietly as Elias knelt to gentle his horse and used his long dagger to put his horse to rest. His men eyeing the event somberly dismounted and walked to him.

"See to yer wounds," Elias nodded to them, before trudging up the slope himself, his breath fogging. Almost casually, he shot an arrow into the back of the last survivor, who had been trying to drag himself away, leaving a blood-red streak in the white snow. Laying behind the fallen mercenaries, he found them—two snow-covered partisan scout corpses.

Elias spit into the colored snow, mumbling a heated curse.

119

"Come hither," he called to his men, half running downhill. "Lend me a horse." He said with command to the nearest rebel.   Mounting and nodding to the two, he continued, "I need return to der Flechtemann, and a hard ride lay ahead. Ye may share the other horse and follow in comfort."

"What be the worry?" the injured man asked, his face grey, a grimace curling his squinting eyes and persed mouth as he spoke.

"Der Flechtemann need know the results of this encounter," Elias muttered. "May it nay be so, but his Yakov, be nay here either and might be lost."

***

Yakov stirred from a fitful sleep, roused by the sounds of a loud commotion. Before he could open his eyes, hands were already upon him. Startled, he stared wide-eyed as a figure roughly pulled him upright, propelling him purposely out of the tent in which he slept.

Yakov fell outside face first in the snow, he scrambled to his feet, his elbows cold and chafed from the fall. The shock of the cold powdery snow drove the last of his sleep from him. He now found himself face to face with two more men. Drinking and eating together, he knew these two after working these last few weeks with them as easy-going mercs, always joking and laughing at bawdy campfire tales. Now, however, their faces grim, they did not meet his gaze.

"What…what be happenin'?" Yakov's voice unnaturally high-pitched to his own ears, now laced with confusion. The mercenaries remained silent, shifting uncomfortably as the third man emerged from his tent.

120

Yakov recognized him as Dumas, a cold and unwelcoming man of few words.

"Dumas? What be this?" Yakov sputtered, a cold certainty running down his back. "Tell me wha' this is. What have I done?"

Pleading for answers he received no response. Yakov's heart raced as Dumas nodded at him to follow. As Yakov took his first tentative step, he realized where he was being led—to the Chain's blood red pavilion, right in the center of the camp.

In that moment, everything grew clear—*the Chain knew*.

Yakov knew the chance to reason, to plead, to talk with any of them would reap no reward of release. The only person who could grant such a boon would be the man in that garish tent, a man with the humorless grin of a wolf and the eyes of a vulture. He steeled himself as best he could as they guided him towards Petres' tent, the quiet of the camp punctuated by mercenaries and soldiers, peering from their tents, or standing, arms crossed, as if paying witness. Some hawked spittle nearby, looking at him with hostile glares. Others gave him a sympathetic glance, before ignoring him as best they could.

Dumas strode forward, parting the tentflap for Yakov to enter. Yakov hesitated as he saw the gaping maw before him, then gulped and stepped forward.

As he entered the dimly lit tent, he could immediately feel the weight of Petres' malignance. A grimy, flickering lamp cast eerie shadows on the walls, enlarging the Chain's shadow so it appeared to sprawl against the canopy of the pavilion like a winged dragon. Tearing his eyes from the unnerving darkness, Yakov's gaze met Petres', and a chill ran

121

down his spine. The grin, thin and menacing, seen by Yakov too many times before, was the grin of a predator reveling in the suffering of its prey.

At Petres' feet lay Mikkel, bound and bleeding, a pitiful sight that stirred a mixture of guilt and fury within Yakov. His friend's hair, tousled and matted, and a mask of blood splattered across his face from a shattered nose. His eyes were nearly swollen shut, bruised a deep purple, and his breathing seemed labored.

Above him, the Chain's eyes gleamed with malice, his war hammer held comfortably on his shoulder. The obvious enjoyment of the torture inflicted upon Mikkel rest squarely in the Cheshire smile he cast in Yakov's direction. The partisan spy knew to navigate this situation with caution lest he be lost to the cause. Even so, the sight before him of his friend's suffering twisted in his gut. He drew in a breath as he soaked in the added despise deepening afresh the hate he felt for Petres.

I must fix this. I must save him, Yakov thought with anticipation.

You can't save him, Satin, sitting on his shoulder whispered. *You can't even save yourself.*

Suppressing the dark voice, Yakov maintained a stoic facade, refusing to give Petres the satisfaction of witnessing his terror. Yet his heart was pounding against his chest like a trapped animal, desperately seeking escape.

Petres's gaze now flicked between Yakov and Mikkel, as if looking for some reaction.

"Y'kuh?" Mikkel mumbled through swollen lips, barely moving.

122

"I be here, Mikkel," Yakov reassured, his lips numb.

"Good of ye t'join us, Yakov," Petres smiled casually, as if discussing the weather.

"There...be some mistake," Yakov stammered, then continuing through deep breaths and a beating heart which felt as if it would leap out of his chest. "I know not why ye have me here, or why Mikkel...?"

The Chain toyed with his war hammer idly, passing it from hand to hand. "Ah, so ye has no inklin' as to what this is?"

"Nay," Yakov said, acting as firm as he could.

"Well, well, Yakov," Petres smiled, as if delighted. "How sweetly ye lie! But I know—I know ye thought ye could play both sides. I know ye be with those accursed insects crawling in the night. For days now, if nay a bit longer, have we been followed—stealthily followed by a pair o' hooded scouts, clearly of rebel sort."

"It be true that I am suspect," Yakov argued, his heart racing. "But how should you know that it be I, aside from feelin' and instinct? Yer men fight for coin. Mayhaps one of them has turned?" He reasoned.

Petres sighed with agitation. "Does ye think me a fool, Yakov?" the Chained snarled. "I knew something be amiss when I see how readily yon rebels knew our plan. How could they know we be headin' north-east? For our path be known only t'me, thee, and yer comrade Mikkel here."

Yakov's heart sank into the anxiety of a captive. The ruse, however clever, he now found himself caught; therefore, no point would suffice in denying his deception now.

123

"Y'thought ye could deceive us, did ye?" Petres accused, a mad glint in his eyes. "Oh, ye think ye be smart, but I suspected thee from the moment ye returned—but then, I wonder'd if ye be strong enough t'be as ruthless as a spy must be, a *good man* such as ye." The Chain acclaimed with cynicism. "But here thou art! Betraying the very folk who gave ye shelter, food, and hearth." Now raising the volume of his voice as he turned and leaned toward Yakov, face to face. "Betraying the very friend who came t'me, vouchin' for yer life. Y'slept among us as a devil fer days, and we none the wiser! Ah, Yakov, it grieves me t'be so, but I be right. There be no innocent soul on this accursed earth."

Yakov's stomach churned, his fists tightening at his sides. The guilt weighed heavily on him, yet defiance still burned within his eyes.

"I…I did wha' I had to," Yakov finally said, his voice steady despite the feelings raging within him. If he could not deny his involvement, he could at least make up an excuse. "Ye knows not, fer I had nay choice. They threatened mine family. But listen, Mikkel had naught t'do with it. I acted on mine own."

Petres gafawed loudly, the twisted sound resonating through the tent. Those who witnessed the event took a half step backward hoping to avoid the Chain's rath. "Ah, such a noble excuse! An' such a feeble 'un, all t'justify yer treachery." Now retreating to a softer more civil accusation he continued. "I made excuses just as those when I be young—oh, how I would yell to myself! *They made me kill! Nay, nay t'were the devil in me that let loose,* says I screemin'. But in the end, dear Yakov—in the end I saw. Then, I knew, there be no devil. There be only I standin' alone, accountin' fer myself."

"Please," Yakov whispered.

124

"Yer words mean nothin' now, to me or to yer friend. I know he knew not of yer sneakin', but that matters not. What matters, Yakov, is the contempt ye has shown me!" the Chain roared, lunging forward to viciously strike at Yakov with the butt of his war hammer. The end of the wooden handle creased the side of Yakov's head, the grain of the wood tearing a ragged cut across his scalp laying open a flap of skin and hair as he fell to the hard ground. Bright red blood oozed freely from the wound mixing with dirt and matting his hair as it ran into his eyes. Laying exposed to the furry of the mercenary leader's attack, the Chain's boot immediately stamped his chest. Yakov felt a rib snap with excruciating pain. The enraged assault by Petres became brutle, with no control or remorse, as Yakov attempted to pull back from the blows.

Breathless, he looked up at the Chain as the man circled around. "It be nothin' personal, Yakov," Petres said, now calm, but displaying malice behind his gaze. "Ye must simply pay fer your deceit." He paused for emphasis and then continued with addendum. "And as must yer friend."

Yakov's gaze from his prone position, shifted towards Mikkel sprawled on the floor nearby as well. Their eyes met, and Mikkel looked toward him with a gaze filled with confusion and pain.

"Petres…I…beg thee," Yakov pleaded, gasping to breathe. "There…be an innocent here…and he be Mikkel. He is innocent. Please….spare him the anguish of your accusations."

Petres' inclined his head. "Perhaps I shall. But the truth this time, friend Yakov. Tell us both who ye be. Tell us what ye passed on." Two guards pulled Yakov upright.

125

"I…" Yakov began weakly. "I came at…the behest o' the rebels…I was to infiltrate myself back into yer lot…'

That so? Quarried the Chain.

Yakov became silent. Anger coming from the leader of the delay, his prisoner received a cuff from one of the guards. Petres continued asking how Yakov and the others communicated?"

Yakov, with bleeding libs began to speak again. "We left signs fer the scouts…I contacted them. I…" his voice faltered as he looked at Mikkel's pained gaze. "…I passed all as best I could."

"And what of yer reason?" the Chain asked, his voice dangerously low. "Was it fer yer old mother, mayhaps? Or a widow'd sister, or a bent up, cripple father? Or has ye more lies t'tell me?" Now pumped up by his on pompacity for having caught the traitor, he sought affirming faces of his men.

Yakov took a shuddering breath, shutting his eyes. "Nay, I did it…fer the cause. I have seen naught but your cruelty to the villagers around. And my vent is the cause is just. Der Flechtemann be twice, nay, thrice the leader as ye. He shall be the patriot to bring ye down to yer grave."

"Ha!" the Chain laughed loudly for all to hear. "There it be—so that is what ye be. A man with ideals, aye, a man with great beliefs. However, Ye be worse, far worse a man than me. While I have lived as an animal, aye, true, I never turned coat friend." Now, examining Yakov's friend he asked, "And what does ye think of him, Mikkel? What do ye think of yer dear friend?"

The hurt in Mikkel's eyes needed no words.

126

"As a traitor," Petres said, suddenly solemn. "Ye shall suffer, Yakov."

"Nay hold back then," Yakov challenged coughing. "Kill me." He continued, blood running from his lips and teeth, his vision blurred from the Chain's blow to his head, and blood and dirt now caked to his cheek. "It is well! End this cud. I be tired, so damned tired. End me, so I can be free of ilk such as ye!"

"Nay," the Chain said. "I shall do worse."

Yakov watched as Petres raised his war hammer, ready to strike—and then his glance flicked to Mikkel. The Chain nodded to himself, and just then, Yakov's eyes widened in horror as he realized what was about to happen. He scrambled forward, on his knees, his movements sluggish, trying to get to Mikkel before—

Without a moment's hesitation, Petres swung the weapon, ending Mikkel's life in a single, brutal blow. The crack of Mikkel's skull shattering between the hammer and the ground echoed in the tent. Blood and bodily matter scattered all around landing on Yakov and those nearest to the deed.

Yakov's stopped and stared with abrupt incredulity at the scene before him.

Everything stopped—there was no more breath to take, no more things to imagine, no more smiles to share. Red-black blood pooled around the remainders of Mikkel's shocked face, flickering in the dim light. Yakov could not breathe. The glassy opaqueness of Mikkel's sightless eyes was something seen by Yakov too often, again and again, battlefield after battlefield—and yet, here it was, that strange, alien, vacant expression, now enshrined upon the pale, shattered visage of his oldest friend.

127

What could have been done to save him? said that cold voice within Yakov's stunned mind. *Mikkel was just here and now he is nowhere, and you could not save him… He is gone, and you may yet follow… Give up—you could not save him, and you can not save the others. Surrender, and let go.*

Yakov's muddled mind could not respond to the voice in his mind before Dumas entered the tent. Dimly, he was aware Petres was still talking, perhaps giving instructions to his guards, or perhaps giving orders to Dumas. As Yakov watched, Mikkel's corpse was dragged passed him to the men gathered outside the tent canopy area.

"Why did ye slay him?" Yakov yelled, his voice seeming distant in his thoughts. Tears seeped into his beard, now dripping to the ground.

"Fer yer actions," Petres said, a retort in a mater-of-fact attitude. "He vouched fer thee, y'see. Trusted ye with his life, and fer that promise, he died, to pay a debt."

"And shall I, too, die now?" Yakov asked with quiet directness.

"Nay," the Chain said, dismissively. "Ye shall but suffer—firstly as an example, and secondly, so that ye may tell me about thine der Flechtemann."

"Had ye let Mikkel live, I would have told ye," Yakov said, his jaw clenched and shuddering. "Not now, nay. Do as ye will. I have little to lose."

"And I shall," the Chain promised with a smirk of a smile. Leaning down he continued with a warning, "But ye has much, much more to lose. Y'see, Yakov, one o' the great truths in the world be this—there be nothin' worse than fear and pain. Nothin'. I need no Mikkel to make ye talk, Yakov,

128

fer ye *will* talk—and I have all the time in the world t'make it so."

Grabbing Yakov's arm, the Chain stood up.

"Dumas!" he called, and the burly man entered. "Take this 'un. Bind him in the open snow to a tree."

The man nodded and dragged Yakov outside, where the merciless cold of the snow awaited him. As the Chain watched silently, ropes were wrapped around Yakov's wrists and ankles, with a final cord tied around his neck, binding him to a tree just close enough to the fire to keep him from freezing to death. Yakov still wore his sleeping clothes, unfit for hunching barefoot in the snow, for the events just passed started with him being abruptly pulled from his tent and blankets.

"Good night, friend Yakov!" said the Chain with a mocking bow. "I shall get to know thee better in the morning!"

With this promise, he left. As Yakov lay there, the freezing snow seeping into his sparce clothes, he puzzled over how he could still feel terror—already, all seemed lost. He, indifferent, brave, and stoic in the face of his fate as he was, felt only a dull terror in his head, as hot tears seeped down his face, while his nose, red and swollen from the cold, purported the only pain in the fog of his mind.

Surrender, said a negative voice, whispering temptations and weakeness. *No cause is worth such pain. Surrender the rebels, and he may let thee die. Then, all will be well...*

Nay, Yakov thought forcefully, the thought burning across his retinas like a comet. *Nay, I will not give up. I will nay surrender. I will suffer, but I will live!*

129

As a clear image of Anna, Dieter, and Hans flickered in his mind's eye, he knew survival of the rebel cause, and, too, himself, to be the greatest focus for him now. He would find a way. He would not be bested by Petres the Chain. Despair still threatened to consume him, but he would not give in to thoughts of defeat.

I must live, Yakov repeated to himself. *Mikkel is gone, but I will live.* He reasoned with determination.

***

"…And you lived," whispered Michael Simon, his own eyes wet as his fingers drifted over the ancient parchment.

The words of the horrific account garnered the most complex effort to decipher so far, written in a disorganized, disorienting mix of local dialects and Latin, switching almost on a word to word basis. Again and again, some sentences or phrases would keep repeating, as if written by a maddened, shuddering hand. Ink streaks dragged across the page in places, as if the writer simply trailed off, unaware that his quill-hand was drifting off, maybe simply falling asleep over his journal.

"Jehoshaphat, that was a task," James said, pinching the bridge of his nose. "The ink's gone everywhere, and the coded Latin's inconsistency in these pages on account of how many errors the journalist made makes following extremely difficult."

"Well, he was reliving a traumatic memory," Michael said distantly. He could all but see the old hand that wrote this—the old, palsied hand belonging to a conscript, rebel, informant, and priest.

"Fair enough," James said, shaking his head. "It's…we'll, messed up, on every level. Hopefully, it'll be an easier read in the next few leafs, both emotionally, and transcription-wise. I don't think this water damage seeped into the next few pages."

"It's not water damage," Michael said.

"Hm? But look at these, look here," James said, excitedly pointing vaguely at several distortions on the page, seemingly droplets. "It must have been drizzling, or he spilled a few drops of rosewater on it, or something,"

"Tears, James," Michael said softly. "They're tears."

Chapter X: Things Left Behind

"...and what I leave behind is this book—and in it, I leave myself behind."

-Brother Jakob, circa 1384

Michael could not sleep.

He said goodnight to James a few hours ago, leaving after James asked Michael several times if he were okay. Michael was not entirely sure why, but something in James' expression or mannerism, seemed off.

Though responding to James' quarries, in confirmation he was fine, something niggled at the corner of Michael's mind. He sighed as he turned over in bed yet again the late night soon became early morning, and still he tried to keep his eyes tightly shut. He yawned, perhaps now, sleep would invade his thinking. Of course, sleep would come just in time for some coffee and getting back to work, back to reading about—

Stop it, Michael scolded himself. *You'll never sleep if you keep thinking about it.*

Time continued to pass… now in wakeful slowness.

Michael sighed, staring at the ceiling. He turned his head and his eye fell to the photograph brought with him from home, one he kept with him in every hotel, airplane, and house wherever stayed the night. His wife, Rachel, looked at him from the photograph with a simple, carefree smile.

His mind once more returned to the tear stains on Yakov's journal. As he reached out and grasped Rachel's photograph, Michael found himself musing at the things humans leave behind. It was not just the stories and memories that lingered on, but rather, the very remnants of humanity seemed to persevere. These signs, these artifacts humans left behind, seemed to Michael like breadcrumbs scattered along a winding trail, a silent witness to the chapters of human life.

Staring at Rachel's photograph, Michael marveled at it. Encased in a simple frame, a universe of emotions stood still, held frozen in a single moment. The familiar warmth in her eyes, the subtle curve of her smile—these details were not just pixels on glossy paper, instead they identified portals into another time, the happiest in Michael's life.

The same transformative quality was present in Yakov's journal; after all, this character was what the old monk left behind of himself, his life, and his moment in history. Those tears on that page, however, somehow meant more to Michael than the narrative itself. They were a human remnant, a real, genuine expression of a pain that transcended time and space, just for Michael to feel the inherent emotion.

"No sleep tonight," Michael muttered.

With a sigh, he lifted himself and gathered the old box from its perch above the room's wardrobe. Gingerly placing the ancient box on his desk, Michael retrieved the journal, laying it open.

"You needed someone to listen, Yakov," Michael said to himself sadly. "And I'm here. I'm listening."

133

With that, Michael lit the bedside lamp, spread out his notes, and began to read.

***

Anna sat rigidly on a log across from der Flechtemann's tent cutting wild onions as she watched from the corner of her eye while he deftly fletched an arrow. The camp around them hummed with activity as men chopped wood and others, including the few women and children, went about their chores. Dieter and Sieghart gone early for a hunting trip gave Anna hope they'd find some game— supplies always seemed to be on the edge of running out.

"There be any word on th'soup, lady Anna?" came Nerijus' cheerful voice as he walked nearby. "The lads be mighty puckish these days."

"I'll call ye when it's ready," Anna scowled, and Nerijus raised his hands in surrender.

"Lord, does thee have resembl'nce to my mother," he muttered, before walking away. Der Flechtemann watched the exchange with something close to a smile as he whittled away at the arrow.

"Will ye save Yakov?" Anna's voice suddenly pierced der Flechtemann's rhythmic movements, cold and sharp.

Der Flechtemann paused, his gaze fixed on the arrow in his hands. Instead of answering her directly, he began to speak.

"Will ye not call me father?" he said in a low voice.

134

"What father?" Anna said bitterly, wiping a tear with her shoulder as she continued to cut the onions. "Mine father be Hans Symon, an' he left long ago."

"I still be Hans, aye, though hidden deep within," he said heavily, the weight of memories etched in the lines across his weathered face. "Just a man like many another man, with a family an' dreams. Such dreams—and then came the call, and I heard in the reason given me fate. I heard that song o' rebellion in some damned tavern." He paused then continued, "I forgot which, ha! Possibly one tankard too many… Imagine that. I heard a song, and I knew what I wanted. An' so I left, convinc'd it be for a greater good. So solid be my faith in tha' decision." Now looking in Anna's direction. "I did it fer you all, so certain…"

Anna's eyes shot towards him, her impatience simmering beneath the surface, little interest in his self-reflection. All she could feel was a burning desire for her brother's safety.

"And the years passed," Der Flechtemann continued, "I did nay look back. I buried me regret like me dead comrades—for six of us rode out together, and of those six, only I remain above the soiled earth. I fought, and I saw dreams die. I saw reality bludgeon man after man. Their faces long gone, and too, the songs we sang in a tavern one drunken night. But aye, I did me best fer their sake, fer the sake o' those who once believed in our cause so fervently. Then one night, as I wondered if I made the right choice, if the sacrifice be worth the cost—those faces emerged out of my concious fog and they reminded me of the decisions made on that night so long ago: *ye chose the cause, and the cause is all ye'll have.*"

Anger flickered in Anna's cold eyes. Holding the knife, used to cut the onions, she pointed it towards her

135

father like a finger of accusation and continued with a raise of her voice.

"Ye speak too much fer a man who *left us.* Talk nay to me o' sacrifice. I've seen this camp. I've seen tha' folk here have families about. Ye simply chose nay to bring us. Ye *chose* to be alone."

For just a moment der Flechtemann's mind flashed to a time long ago when he heard the stern scolding from his Olga, their mother, his wife, now long dead. *How like her,* he thought. Slowly the reverie of the remembrance faded, and his focus came back to Anna's intense voice.

He shot her a concerned look not knowing exactly what to say. His words failed before her cold gaze. Remembering again the words between he and his wife on his decision to leave, Anna's father tried to explain. "I thought ye'd be cared for…I never expected…"

"That yer fool of a brother, Karl, wouldst be a fool, a drunkard, a snake?" Anna scoffed.

"Aye," der Flechtemann said softly, looking away. "That's what I'd made meself believe. In the darkness of night as I lay in bed, next to dear Olga, I reasoned with sweet lies to me thoughts. When me heart beat like a taught strung bow thrummed at the pluck, I simply let fly. I convinced me soul all was well for our blood, that I'd chosen rightly." Pausing briefly, then continuing, "Why should me wife be soaked in blood by me side? Why should me sons endure such hardship? What call provided me the right to cause me daughter to crawl through muck beside me? I fed all these notions to me heart, and only then, and in nay another way, could I find solace. Only then could I keep on living."

"An' yet here I am," Anna said in a quiet, dark voice. "Yer own blood, mud-drenched. Yer son is taken; yer wife long-gone. What use were thy lies?"

Again, der Flechtemann fell silent. Anna leaned forward, her eyes alight and with as much quiet, direct emphasis as possible she said, "Now spare me this, ye knows mine brother be dragged off t'some castle, where he shall suffer behind wood an' stone. Only now have ye a chance while the Chain strides through the open. Ye must take it. Does ye understand, father? *I want mine brother back.*"

"And ye shall have him," der Flechtemann said grimly. The pointed bitterness behind the word *father* was not lost on him. Behind his mask of stone, another crack appeared on a jaded heart. "And know all I shall do, I shall do fer thee."

She did not respond, returning to the onions and soup. They sat in silence, his hands still working on the arrow, scraping away strips so the balance of the projectile held true and fly without fault. He thought of many things as he worked, a trait of his thinking used for many years—but today, all he could think of was the day he left his family the first time, and, too, remembering a time before that, the day last seeing any vestige of warmth in his daughter's eyes.

For her part, Anna called the men to eat and began to hand out bowls to those without the comfort of family, she was lost in her role as a mother of sorts, a carer and provider—she allowed herself to joke and scold and slap at hands too eager to wait for their share. What she did not do was to look back at der Flechtemann, at the face who reminded her, all too much, of a smiling father who disappeared in the night.

137

For Yakov, a chill of despair ate at the very fiber of his being prodded on by a cold wind as it howled over the plains. Only an hour or two since sunset with camp set, Yakov rested as best he could. Dragged behind the mercenary procession for the past weeks, his hands tied to the back of a cart, exhausted limbs struggled to keep pace. The practice of tormenting the prisoner took many forms, being pelted with small rocks to get a reaction from him appeared to be the favorite pastime of most of the mercenaries. Although some were kind enough to secretly offer him water while attempting not to be caught doing so.

Now in the dark, Yakov again bound tightly to a makeshift post at the edge of the mercenary camp, spent the cold nights staring out into the abyss of nothingness. His body weight suffering, cold seeped into his jutting bones. Too his hair unwashed, and his unkempt beard were caked with dried blood. His eyes, their luster lost, yet hope remained and even in their sickly yellow, a spark remained—a hint of fire Petres the Chain continued to attempt to extinguish day after day, week after week.

As Yakov coughed, hawking phlegm onto the barren earth, his body ached with every contraction. Every joint screamed in protest. Bloodstained bindings cut into his wrists, a cruel reminder of futile struggles to get free. The Chain allowed him the remnants of a tattered cloak, which now clung to his battered frame, making for an ill shield against the cold. The campfire flickered much too far in the distance requiring him to stretch and strain to catch some warmth with the bare toes poking through boots warn thin with constantly being dragged behind a wagon.

The grisly memory of Mikkel's death still lingered in the periphery of his mind, though he tried not to think of it. The image of the sight still clung to his eyes whenever he shut them.

Petres reveled in tormenting Yakov. The relentless beatings with searing pain were etched into his mind—yet, through the haze of agony, Yakov still clung to the fragments of his will. Any shallow sleep he happened to come by now resulted in muttering to himself or a plea of dreams.

And for what? What can ye do? came the voice, familiar now. *He'll come soon, ye can beg him to make death come quick.*

"Ye can't break me…an' nor can he," Yakov mumbled through cracked lips, defiance in his hoarse whisper.

Oh, give up. There's nay escape, naught a hope, and so who will come for ye now?

"The rebels—me father. I be of them, and they will remember."

Will they? Or have they simply left ye behind?

Yakov shook his head vehemently, then stilled as a nearby sentry looked at him strangely.

"Traitor's losin' it," the man called out to one of the other mercenaries with a laugh. "Tossin' his head like yon hounds a howlin'."

A bark of distant laughter abruptly interrupted Yakov. Responding to some inner awareness he remained still, no longer listening to the voices inside him. Hardship was not foreign to him, and this outburst of insults would not shake him. He would not yield to this nightmare, not now. A

139

battleground of memories swirled within his mind, for he a soldier. His rememberances of family, his spear, and his shield now became his cause never to be surrendered to any interloper. The thought of Anna, Dieter, and the rebels swirled in his mind as a makeshift family in their shared struggle. He pictured their faces, imagined their voices, and drew strength from them.

Hours seemed to pass, though time mattered little. Through the haze of pain and exhaustion, Yakov's eyes made out the visage of a figure approaching. As the wind whispered through the barren landscape, he could hear the familiar, heavy footfall of Petres the Chain.

Petres looked down, unsmiling now, his eyes as dead as the earth. No joy shown there, no hate, no love, no hunger—nothing. They were the eyes of a fish, or of some kraken from a sailor's tale, and Yakov thought he now understood Petres. He understood that underneath so much, underneath the smiles and the hunting hunger, underneath the raging, laughing, monstrous hound, was…nothing. He was hollow. Yakov—bruised, beaten, and bloodied as he was, almost pitied his tormentor.

"And shall ye loosen yer tongue tonight?" Petres asked, a hint of trite resignation in his voice.

Yakov slowly shook his head.

"I thought not, friend," Petres sighed, musing as he produced a wooden baton. "And so, we start anew."

And then there was pain. Yakov knew, this time, it could not break him.

Chapter XI: First Blow

"Who counted back to the first blow? I kill him for he killed my father for he killed his father…and so on; and sins breed sins, and monsters multiply. Kingdom blames kingdom; each monster a victim, each victim a monster to be…and if you ask Caine why he killed, [shall] he not say, Nay, I struck not the first blow…"

-Brother Jakob, circa 1384

Dawn painted the sky with hues of blood and gold as Elias, taciturn as ever, gathered his forces on the outskirts of the mercenary camp. He stifled a yawn as he looked around him. The crisp morning air hung with anticipation as the mounted contingent of a dozen rebels, their faces cloaked, readied their bows astride their horses. The idea of an always moving mounted archery, though not new to some, made the tactical appearance with the tribes of the far eastern plains eons of time before. The handing of the battle tactic from warrior chief to generals over the centuries brought the concept of any advantage to those who would take the time to learn. The skill, however, did not always work well in the mountains of der Flechtemann's homeland, but enamored with the idea, der Flecthemann and Elias worked diligently to include the ability to deliver a blow using this hit and run tactic.

"Elias," came a voice. Elias turned in his saddle to see one of the scouts.

"What be it, man?"

"Sieg be sendin' word. His scouts over yon hill ha' told him the enemy is up an' breakin' their fast."

"Aye, then 'tis time," Elias whispered to his eager mare as he spurred the nervous war horse to face the mounted partisan fighters. Standing in his saddle he commanded, "Listen, friends—be quick and fierce, for we must move like an arrow smooth as silk through the enemy camp, 'round them wide on the flank, circling, ever circling, deftly finding your targets. Be ye like wraiths in the attack. Then, as the whistle of an arrow's fletch in flight, on me signal, be gone. Strike fear quickly, and naught of ye be stragglers, ken me? When we return to der Flechtemann, himself, there be not a drop o' thy blood on thine saddles. Aye?"

The men nodded, quietly affirming Elias entreaty with their plaudits and huzzas. Pleased at what he saw and heard, Elias nodded back, gratified by the unsentimental nature of his contingent, unlike the jabs and barbs traded by Sieghart's lot. A clean structure of command always appealed to him.

"Form up and follow mine lead," he ordered, taking the head of the v-shaped formation. As they cantered in open ground up the hill hiding them from the Chain's camp. At the walk the mercenary camp slowly came into view. Dark silhouettes of still-unpacked tents and flickering campfires contrasted against the emerging light. Elias now encouraging a cantor, clenched his jaw. *We now disturb their sleep, these monstrous men?* He reflected. *How dare they rest easy, for the pain they inflict on the unskilled villager and farmer?*

He inclined his head towards his men, his eyes hard.

"Listen—aim fer the hounds. At the gallup now," he shouted.

The men hesitated for a moment, then nodded back. Their war cries sounding over the field of contest. War was war, and their commander was a man forged in the crucible of rebellion. Now standing in his sturrups and leaning forward while he raised his bow, his swift horse racing towards the enemy camp, Elias signaled the rebels to ready their bows as they made their charge.

As the first shard of dawn burst upon the horizon like bleeding glass, Elias spurred his horse ever forward, leading the charge of rebels. The thud of hooves against the cold, hardened ground echoed like a distant war drum. Immediately, the hounds were barking, and the mercenaries were startled to find any alert posture, Yelps and disparate warhorns resounded discordantly, the rebels generating confusion in their adversary as they rode through the assembly of tents and then turned to flank of the mercenary camp, riding in a storming circle, arrows notched, bows ready.

Breathing in, Elias gave the shrill call of a bird—the signal. The first volley of arrows soared through the chilly air, and immediately, the mercenary camp now in total chaos arrows found their marks, piercing the stillness with screams of surprise and alarm. More than half the arrows struck the barking dogs their howls turned into gurgling whines.

Aim and fire, the order given by der Flechtemann to Elias. He did not want a stray arrow embedded in his son's throat. Each projectile must count, but at no cost to the rebels.

Some of the mercenary sentries pelted the patriots with slings, but the stones whistled past harmlessly. The rebels, their faces concealed beneath the hoods of their cloaks, remained elusive on horseback. Again, their bows sang in unison, delivering a relentless onslaught from

143

multiple directions. The element of surprise was their ally, and they exploited it with deadly precision—a sentry fell from his perch on a rock, an arrow between his surprised eyes.

Other mercenaries, tearing through their tents, fumbled for weapons. Despite the disarray, Elias witnessed the depth of discipline of the Chain's men. Most likely, Yakov's rescue fell close to the thoughts of the mercenary commanders; however,—unfortunately for the mercs, this was not der Flechtemann's objective.

Not yet.

Screams continued as arrows continued to rain down, finding vulnerable points within the camp. Elias prodded the rebels on with calculated precision, the cold dawn air biting into his skin as he spurred his horse forward. He led the rebels with a calculating gaze, and as tents flapped in the brisk wind, their emerging occupants fell shrieking, arrows protruding from their shoulders and collarbones.

Elias continued to signal to his men, directing their arrows towards key targets—anyone who seemed important.

The Chain's men were already regrouping, shields up, retaliatory arrows whistling through the air. But Elias his objective completed successfully unsettled the mercenaries, sowing doubt within their ranks. A swift and brutal raid would send a message—the rebels were still a formidable force, and the mercenaries now became the hunted.

Arrows flew through the dawn from both sides now, and Elias took as many shots at the enemy cavalrymen as he could before the mercenaries could reach their own mounts. The wounded enemy fell into turgid crawls, creating a bloody tableau of brutality on the snow-dusted earth—but already, their comrades were sprinting past them. A final

144

arrow from Elias' bow buried itself into the skull of a cavalry man mid-mount. Elias then turned and called again, louder, his pitch higher this time—signaling retreat.

The raid achieved its purpose.

Hearing Elias signal, their faces concealed by hoods, the rebels, began their swift retreat. Hounds and cavalrymen attempted to keep pace, only to shy away as more arrows flew past. Soon, anxious not to let his men get drawn out for fear of a trap, the Chain called the chase off. The mercenaries reluctantly broke off their pursuit. Elias and the rebels flew into the wilderness, quickly disappearing just as they earlier attacked the mercs. A regrouping of the patriots soon took place by a stream nearby, prearranged between der Flechtemann and Elias.

As they dismounted they drank deeply from their thirst and washed their faces in the icy water. Elias took a draught of it and nodded at his men.

"Good showin', friends," he said, before glancing at one in particular. "Injured?" He inquired looking into the man's eyes.

"Nay, only a scratch. A swine's sling-swung stone caught me leg," the man grumbled.

"Worry not. Ride back to camp and ask them to send another warrior in yer place."

"Aye," the man nodded, clearly disappointed as he winced to stand. "What shall I say in me report t'der Flechtemann?"

"Tell him we have struck the first blow," Elias said with a grim smile.

145

"The first blow," Sieghart grumbled as the injured man stopped his report. He sat in der Flechtemann's tent, beside the rebel leader himself and Nerijus. "What first blow? We've suffered from the min'strations of yon snakelike mercenaries fer months now."

"He means the first o' this plan," Der Flechtemann said.

"Oh aye," Nerijus nodded, before raising a hand to gain attention. "'Cept, o'course, ye have nay explained the plan."

Der Flechtemann sighed with subtle irratation at having to explain himself. "Suffice it t'say Elias will be busy o'er the next weeks. He shall harm and harry the enemy, though I doubt he shall have this much success again. The Chain is nay a fool. Precautions shall double, if naught, triple."

"Why 'im?" Sieghart frowned, sulking. "Why Elias? Ye could have sent either I or Nerijus—so why send the skulker off t'battle? Have this thickhead or I failed ye in somethin'? "

"Nay, but speak t'me when either of ye can shoot from the saddle," der Flechtemann said drily, noting their annoyed expressions. "Aye, see—I play no favorites among ye, so be not children. I sent 'im, fer he be the man fer the job."

"Well, Now I know the plan," Nerijus affirmed somewhat uneasy and feeling a bit left out of the planning., "—but what shall it accomplish?" He paused, eyeing der

146

Flechtemann. "Should we nay freed good Yakov when the chance be in our favor?"

"Nay, fer Petres knew he was bein' trailed," der Flechtemann responded. "Most likely, his men were packed close 'round wherever our Yakov be bound, prepared just for a desperate rescue. Had our attack ventured into their camp proper, barely a man would have survived."

"Then, first blow made," Sieghart said, leaning forward with simple interest. "What do we do next?"

"We move camp further along," der Flechtemann said. "To some leagues t'the north-west, there be a fine old forrest, hill-struck and brambled. There shall we set camp, and entrench ourselves so the enemy may find us."

"What?" Nerijus asked in alarmed horror—a ghostly pale coming over his face. "Would ye have us besieged…? Nay, sir, I cannot stomach it—nay. I have lived through a siege once, and t'would have been a mercy to die 'nit. I'd die before livin' through another blasted siege, much less one where I'm freezin' mine backside on rocks an' dirt…"

Much to his surprise der Flechtemann was smiling slightly at this outburst. Too late, Nerijus realized something was afoot.

"…but ye have a plan, thinks I," he added sheepishly.

"An' so I do," der Flechtemann said, and Sieghart nodded. They still did not know what the rebel leader was planning, encouraged but somewhat skeptical the two differed to the leadership once again.

***

"Yer lot did this," said the youth, bitterly.

Yakov stared at the corpses burning nearby blankly, before looking back at the tearstained face of the young man. He was short of height, his red hair choppily cut, freckles covering his face. He wore the tattered gambeson of a conscript, and though he looked nothing like him, he reminded Yakov strangely of a young Mikkel.

"I said, yer lot did this," the youth repeated, sobbing, now angrily pointing at the pyre. "My friend be in tha'. He be dead, all the arrows of yer lot." He spat with vehemence onto the ground near where Yakov sat tied to a tree. "Damn ye traitor."

Yakov remained quiet as the youth cried again. Around him, he could feel the dark gaze of several of the mercenaries, and knew many of them would have him dead if it were up to them. However, the Chain made his wishes quite clear, no one was to touch Yakov.

Except, of course, him.

"Yer lot did this to us," the young man once more spat towards Yakov between sobs, his body quaking in anger. "We'll have yer skins. Ye'll see."

"Quit yer blubberin'," one of the men muttered, then giving Yakov a hard look. "But the lad's right, traitor. Yer lot should've run when they could. Now, they will die. Petres doesn't ferget."

"Ye chased us," Yakov rasped. "We didn't…we were only…"

"Ye shot our lot half-dead in an ambush," the man said shortly. "And now again, ours have died in a second

148

ruse. Aye, we are fightin' men—and aye, die'n be in our writ. But we are men, and we hate where needed. Take heed, our hate is now true and just."

Yakov, quieted now, stared patiently at the youth, still, though, he did not understand. This youth before him, looked with dark vacant eyes to some abstract, warped justification for the Chain's actions. Yakov, once almost put under the same spell, now was quite aware of the fear Petres and his cohorts put over on these unsuspecting young recruits. He looked at the crying youth and this time, he saw himself, crying for a lost friend. How alike they were, and for a moment Yakov wanted to reason with the youth, to explain, to tell him about his friend, Mikkel…

…Mikkel what? He thought exasperated with anger. *Mikkel became nothing but a regrettable casualty, just a conscript at the wrong place in the wrong time, minding the dogs on the wrong watch…. His task to guard no different than any other soldier past or present, asked to stand in any similar situation in the pattern of time…* and so Yakov made the leap of thought, *patterns in life repeated themselves, and even if this young man and he felt the same pain, they could not connect.*

That night, sleep did not come easy—waking before dawn, he could hear the ragged breathing of a young voice behind him. Yakov froze, then, something fell to the earth with a hard thud, and the breathing faded. Finally daring to slowly look back, Yakov found nobody there. Laying on the ground behind him a large stone, large enough to crack a man's head open, sat resting on the hard earth.

Chapter XII: Respect

"...I've seen that man craves above all else respect; he kills for it and dies for it, lives in it or pines for it, [and yet], the fragile beast breaks behind him—and no coaxing can piece it back."

-Brother Jakob, circa 1382

Elias and his men now returning after their latest foray, weary and exhausted, brought with them the injured. Anna passed amongst them with a bucket of water viewing the rebel camp, loud with the commotion of the aftermath of the latest raid. She could see the most recent encounter clearly was less successful than previous raids. There were more wounded, and even Elias himself rubbed some sort of ointment onto his side as he huddled near der Flechtemann, giving his report.

As she hurried as much as she could without spilling the water, she felt a panic in the air, which hung heavy with a strange, acrid scent. The injured rebels lay on makeshift cots, their faces etched with a blend of pain and grim determination.

"Anna! Leave the water, come hither!" came a cry, and Anna immediately set the bucket down before hurrying to the voice.

As she reached the medic's tattered tent, she could see their healer, old Werner bent over one of the wounded, who was struggling. His legs kicked, while his arms were pinned to his side by a hard-faced woman, her dirty blond hair tied in a severe bun that made her look far older than her actual age. She looked in Anna's direction with an urgent gaze as Anna entered the tent.

"I'll 'old the legs!" Werner grunted. "Anna, ye hold his arm so Hilda can burn the wound!" Anna nodded, immediately taking over the woman's task, as Werner shifted his position to try and hold the man's limbs still. The healer, a weathered man with steady hands and a head full of obscure knowledge about herbs and poultices, was today grim-faced.

Anna could see the young soldier laying beneath her grasp, red-haired and wide eyed, biting down on a clumped rag. His clothes stained with blood, and the pungent scent of infection clung to the air all around the space of the tent. A small group of rebels were beginning to gather around, helping Werner keep the man still, their expressions reflecting concern.

Anna, her sleeves rolled up to reveal calloused hands, exchanged an uncertain glance with Hilda. The acrid scent of burning flesh mingled with the unmistakable stench of infection, creating an oppressive atmosphere around the table of operation.

Werner glanced at Anna, his eyes conveying both urgency and reassurance. "Hold his arm firm, lass! An' Hilda, yon blade ought be hot enough anow—fetch it again! Quick, now, quick!"

Hilda nodded, retrieving the hot bar of metal. Anna's gaze, however, fixed on the young man's face where she witnessed the intense fear in his wide eyes. With anxiety a silent plea for relief of searing pain to come awaited his lips. The rag in his mouth muffled his cries, but the agony was etched deeply on his face with the agony of anticipation.

Werner's helper approached with a heated blade, the glow from the hot metal appearing strange in the eerie darkness, blotting out any other light. As the rebels looked on in discomfort, Werner took a deep breath. "Hold steady, lad," he murmured to the wounded rebel, his tone gruff.

An almost inaudible gasp came from the young warrior. As Hilda withdrew the blade, the wounded rebel's body sagged in momentary relief and a partial unconsciousness. The deed done, sweat dripped down his temples as his labored breaths echoed in the tense stillness of the tent. Anna released her grip on his arm, exchanging a weary glance with Hilda.

Werner, though wearied by the relentless demands of his role, met their gazes with a nod of acknowledgment.

"Well done to ye," Werner said.

Glancing towards Anna, Hilda smiled and gently nodded.

"I'll fetch the water now," Anna made to leave, but Werner shook his head.

"Nay, I'll send a lad by," he said. "But be a dear, take mine niece and get her some'in to eat." Glancing to his helper he continued, "No, don't ye be shakin' yer 'ead," he interjected before Hilda could protest. "Off ye go with frau Anna."

"Come," Raising an eyebrow of understanding, Anna encouraged the woman, who again nodded albeit reluctantly.

Further from the medic's camp, the scent of damp earth permeated the air, and above them, a few trees still spread out their leaves, too twisted to be felled.

Perched on a rocky hill in the heart of the woods, this new camp now fortified with other defenses still being constucted. The hill, shaped like a natural mound, provided a strategic advantage with a single ascent leading to the summit. Surrounding the base, the rebels were creating a makeshift barrier using, sharpened to a point, jutting, felled logs and strategically positioned wagons, creating a practical and nearly impenetrable defense against cavalry. Tents and makeshift structures dotted the hill, arranged in a utilitarian manner, shielded in the direction of the entrance by leafy branches thrown over the sides. Two campires flickered—one for the wounded, near the healer's tent, and the central fire, which was Anna's own kingdom.

This new stronghold now built according to der Flechtemann's plans—though whatever they were, Anna could only guess.

Anna led Hilda towards the fire at the center of the camp, far from the injured, where a reduced pot of stew still simmered near hot coals and a flame. Anna filled two bowls then handed one to Hilda.

Hilda glanced at Anna, as they sat on a log near the fire, her expression a mix of gratitude and exhaustion. "Thanks be to ye for helpin'. I know ye already has much to do, like cookin' for all yon oafs around us."

Anna cast a smirk of a smile towards Hilda. "Oafs, aye, they eat like horses, these 'uns. But nay worry. We all do what we ought to 'round 'ere. Including the welcomed help ye give t'yer uncle."

"Aye," Hilda said easily, accepting a bowl of soup. "'T'as been easier to grow among these folk, far from the trappin' o' class or creed. Men, women, afforded no difference in station of use."

Anna nodded. "Even now, that ain't a thing I'm used to hearin'. Back among the villages and towns and such, we'd be doin' little more than tillin' land or birthing babes."

Hilda chuckled with a young woman's newfound wisdom. "Aye, well, this be not that world—though t'hear Da talk, the mission be t'make that world like the one 'ere. With this lot, we be all just tryin' to survive. Man, woman—don'ay matter. We all bleed the same, fight the same." She paused, "Besides, I don'ay think I could stand livin' on some farm, waitin' to pop a bairn."

Hilda took a cautious sip of the stew, the warmth of the broth offering a momentary respite. Anna looked at her. "Ye grew up amongst this lot, aye!"

"Aye," Hilda nodded. "And der Flechtemann don'ay care if ye be a man or a woman. Long as ye can earn yer keep and got the heart to struggle, ye be welcome here. I help me Da most days."

"I've seen ye," Anna said, ignoring the mention of her father. "Just never been much fer speakin'. Wha' be yer years lass?"

"Aye, ye kept to yerself," Hilda nodded, then responding to Anna's question, "I have eighteen summers behind me." Hilda affirmed with pride, a curious glance toward Anna and continuing, "Old enough to know which end of the spear be sharp," She chuckled taking another taste of the soup. "And," she continued with a smirk, "old enough to keep a man happy."

Anna quietly laughed, images of Sieghart coming to awareness. A long pause followed with both women staring into the fire. Hilda, her thoughts gathered, spoke once more, "Simple enough in me mind ta be in comfort here," she shrugged. "Respect the folk around ye, that be all it takes—be they man or woman, folk 'er' folk."

Anna could not help but smile at Hilda's wisdom, such a simple remark, and yet so true—only upon following Sieghart and joining this camp did she first experience respect as a person, not just as a dependent for care, nor expectation for futures in which she found no interest. And though her feelings for her father remained strained, she could not help but respect this shift in rational ideals he fought to create in the shadow of his cause, one that appealed to her more than anything else.

***

"Our lads followed 'em up this time," the mercenary named Dumas brashly said, crossarmed as he reported to the Chain.

The mercenary leader nodded, reclining on a rough wooden chair by the warming fire, his gaze distant. Red unruly hair tied back, he carefully gave himself a shave with the keen edge of his newly sharpened knife. Though he would allow his aide to sharpen the blade, he shuddered to think what would happen if he allowed any of his men near his throat. Instead, he dabbed the fire-warmed water across his stubbled face before scraping at his cheeks with the whetted knife.

Nearby, Yakov sat bound to a tree, gaunt and haggard, his hands and feet shackled together with leather

155

thongs, a stout rope around his arms and chest. He looked at the proceedings through a curtain of shaggy hair. His hairline unevenly altered by a deep scar on the side of his head where his hair grew back slowly leaving the appearance of an unusual part when combed. The pain of the wound's scar given to him by the edge of the Chain's war hammer, reminded him of his young friend Mikkel, cruely killed by Petres.

"And?" Petres queried, pausing his shave momentarily.

"We 'ave em," Dumas said in his typically flat tone. "The rebels be holed up in some owl-plucked, mud-caked forest not too far from here. A base of some sort, thinks I, for the reports mention more than one trail of camp-smoke from the foot o' hill they be entrenched near."

"Entrenched," the Chain slowly said, his brow furrowing. He shot a sidewise glance at Yakov. "Well Yakov, that be real strange-like. Yer folks don't do much entrenchin', now, do they?" He continued, pointing the shaving knife at Yakov. "Nay, they buzz like gnats in mine ear. Why entrench, and lose their mobility?"

Yakov did not reply. Dumas, however, spoke up. "I—well, the men, really—the scouts and I were thinkin'…"

"Yer not paid t'think, be ye?" Petres raised a bushy eyebrow, his tone sardonic. "But pray tell, Dumas, what yon scholar-folk ha' ascertained. What bright ideas ha' ye brought me?"

Now a bit hesitantly, Dumas ventured to talk in a more assured manner. "The men…" he paused to take

156

measure of Petres and continued, "and I, of course, be thinkin' it might be time fer pitched battle," Dumas said, spreading his arms. "Fer see around ye, sir, we are exhausted from this damned hunt, and morale falters. If them bastard-folk keep shootin' arrows in the night burnin' our supply wagons, hunger an' nerves shall do what three dozen knights could not. Spirits would fail, and ye shall have a mutiny on thy hands."

"Who from?" Petres barked, not flinching as his knife nicked his proffered cheek. A bead of blood rolled slowly down his face as he stared at Dumas. Quickly grabbing the linen cloth he used as a washcloth, he daubed at the blood while squinting at his scout and asked with calculated accusation, "And shall ye be the mutineer?"

"Be I or some other," Dumas replied quietly with reserved contemplation. "Ye knows it does nay matter. We came out t'hunt, and now we sent the quarry a-scurry, guts-hangin', to its den. Though we spied more than one campfire, but their spread be sparse. I reckon they lost more men in yon mountains than our folk, t'frost or hunger, as it may be. These raids have been their solace, true, but their spirits must be low." He paused looking at Petres. With a little more confidence, he reinforced his manner with more intent in his delivery. "This be the time t'push advantage, and ye ought know it. If we let this be—" Cut off with a waive of a hand by the Chain, Dumas stepped back in caution.

"Yer point is made," Petres hissed, his knuckles white around the knife. "Now be off afore I gut ye. Ye shall have me decision shortly."

Dumas nodded, exhaling as he walked away. Looking at the man's worry-lined face, Yakov knew under his tough exterior, even this hardened mercenary was afraid of the Chain—they all were. Yet fear could only go so far, and Yakov instinctively knew, if it came to it, Dumas would indeed be the one leading a mutiny.

"Well well," Petres muttered darkly, toying with his knife. "Yer Fletcher has me cornered, he does—y'see what he's done, Yakov?"

Yakov nodded slightly, wincing at his stiff neck.

"Ye always be smart," Petres said, sighing as he rubbed the blood from his face with the linen cloth still in hand from his morning shave. "The only currency t'matter to a man such as I be respect. Gold, jewels, all come and go, but without respect—aye, without that, a man in mine place is meat. What der Flechtemann has laid fer me is naught but a trap. He awaits like a grinnin' lion in a cave— and more fool I, fer I must march in like some idiot yeoman, hungry fer haunches albeit still have steel in 'em. But I canna' lose face now—and so the die is cast, as the nobles say."

The Chain looked at Yakov appraisingly. "Per'aps I should take ye with me—ye must have carers among them rebelfolk, fer ye to remain so silent. Per'aps ye may be of use."

Yakov shifted his position where he sat bound as best he could to allay a cramp causing him discomfort. *Nay,* he thought. *Ye shall not use me, monster.*

Aloud, with feigned amusement, he forced a grim bark of laughter. Petres looked at him quizzically. Yakov returned a half smile.

"If they cared fer my skin, I'd not fester here," he said, trying to sound as bitter as he could. "And fer silence—I have more t'protect than rebels barking at you."

Petres continued to look at him carefully, as though wondering what else Yakov possibly hid. "Curiouser by the minute! Ye've been true-resilient, though a scoundrel ye want t'be, I respect it, but I donna' ha'ta stand it. Ye shall not break with sticks an' fists, think I—and I have not blooded ye much on the road lest yer wound catch rot and bring death. But nay, 'tis settled, ye shall stay the course wi'our lot to the castle." The Chain smiled ruefully looking into Yakov's eyes and continued, "The Pavlović have some o' the best racks I seen. I shall lock thee in one…and then I shall unravel thy story, for sure."

Yakov stayed silent, though his limbs succumbed to the cold from growing fear of a move with the Chain once more and the plight which lay before his sister and brother. Yakov could see no way to intervene. All he could do at the present was stare back into his enemies' eyes.

Petres smirked at his prisoner's silence before making a face as he stood and stretched releasing Yakov from his fixed gaze. Immediately, he put his grin back, turned to his men and bellowed, "Here me, ye brutish, grotty lot! Gather, fer I have a plan to lay before ye—we know where the enemy be, and entrenched as he be, der Flechtemann shall no' flee us in time. Let here be the graves o' yon mangy rebels! Fer every arrow their lot may shoot, let me see one o' their corpses in kind!"

159

The mercenaries, who gathered around their leader, broke out into mottley cheers, while not too far away, Yakov noted Dumas nodding in relief.

Father, Yakov thought, *I hope y'have a plan.*

Chapter XIII: Motte and Bailey

"And have I not seen the castles men have made?

The crenellations, the arrow-slits, the murder-holes and [the spaces] in-between; I have…known the horror of being trapped by walls, to be herded by mortar, to be led and confused and confounded by the minds of men, to have death [rain upon] you even as the sun gleams against the beautiful faccade…

…[And so] is man, beautiful and terrible, cruel and brilliant, and his greatness is matched only by his capacity for the grotesque…"

-Brother Jakob, circa 1384

Carefully, Dieter lowered himself and yet another bushel of straw down the slope, picking his way among the rocks and crags as he held the rope belaying him for support. The incline here was steep, and despite almost slipping twice, he once again reached the bottom safely. Panting, he rested a moment and took time to look around. Here, at the fore of their defenses and new camp, a false camp deception was underway. Many of the barriers now encircled this "advance camp" instead, as well as a fair number of tents. He and others worked hard to move hay and materials down the incline below the primary camp most of their day. Tossing the hay with the rest Dieter stretched his sore arms. Giving a big sigh and looking back up the hill he grimaced at the eventuality of having to climb once more. It seemed too much of the day still lay ahead of him and the rest of the rebels. Simply, he was becoming quite tired.

Hearing something behind him, he turned to see Sieg throw another tent down. Noticing Dieter's tired stance, Sieg offered a grin and waved him over.

"C'mere my friend, then," Sieg said. "I see ye've spent the day up and down this hillock. Rest a bit and help me stand this tent here a-right."

Dieter nodded and lending his hand to another task that needed to be done, together they began work. He saw little of Sieghart around camp recently. Now, in charge of the scouts and hunting parties, Sieg would come into camp to report and spend a precious few minutes or hours with Anna or helping Dieter with some needed tasks. He would then be gone again. Noticing Sieghart's beard thickened some since last together, Dieter could sense in Sieg's eyes some new emotion hanging in his manner…something troublesome…this, even though his demeanor appeared cheerful as they worked.

"Can't understand it," Dieter muttered, making smalltalk. "Why be we makin' this? We set camp atop a hill with a fine view, only to make this cramped, shoddy copy hereat, why?"

"Don't ye see it?" Sieghart said, eyebrows raised. "Right, stand 'ere and look up. Ye see the camp?"

Dieter complied, squinting up."Only the smoke— but the rest, nay, not fer the shrubbery an' the like, but what—" Suddenly it clicked. "Oh."

"Aye," Sieg grinned. "Once we light the flames down 'ere, shift a few folk down…"

162

"It'll seem like this be the only camp," Dieter finished, shaking his head. "Father's layin' a trap." He said in whispered understanding.

"Aye, that he be," Sieg nodded. "He's taken the ol' motte n' bailey castles o' the nobles, and copied their design out o' a mound and planks o' wood. A raised main motte, an' a lower bailey as the entrance, replicated in a forest, bless 'is mind. Never seen a wit quite like yer father's."

"My father…" Dieter muttered. "Sieg?"

"Aye?"

"Shall we live through this?" Dieter asked, looking at the rebel directly. "Trap or no, we play now with a fire o'wit. Shall we burn fer it?"

Sieghart shrugged. "Who be t'say? But yer father has led me through raids would whiten a man's hair, an' still here I stand 'afore ye. So fer now, trust 'em we must, lad. While I stay here, I continue to give him counsel o' care—but fer our gambit in war, only his wit may suffice."

Dieter nodded and felt the crud of anxiety rise in the pit of his stomach as he thought of danger approaching his sister. He wondered, too, of Yakov, out there somewhere in advance of the rebel assembly, and feared for them both. But he also knew, now too was his time…he needed to help.

"Sieg?"

"Aye?"

"I shall fight," Dieter heard himself calmly say. "This time, I shall fight."

Sieg took a long hard look into Dieter's eyes and found there the earnest determination needed in the cause.

163

He remembered der Flechtemann once saying in council, "The younger and wiser men and women will be called upon to lead us forward. Upon them rests a new beginning."

Refocusing Sieghart quietly acknowledged, "Yer sister will kill me fer it—but it be true yer a man. It be yer choice, Dieter. Every man and woman here be a volunteer. If ye wishes to fight—well, I will not stop thee."

Dieter nodded, grateful. There was little he could do in the grand scale of things, and even though he was growing sickened with the life of the rebels, he could not sit idly by while the enemy advanced on the place that, for better or worse, now became his home.

***

Hilda glanced at Anna with a mirth-filled smirk, her eyes sizing up Anna's determined scowl. "All right, my friend. Pull it back again."

Anna squared her shoulders, eyeing the bow in her hands. "Are ye sure it be strung right? Feels like hell t'draw." She said as she struggled to draw the tightly strung bow, arrow nocked. Anna let fly the shaft towards a makeshift target some thirty paces away. The missile died to the ground only achieving two-thirds the distance needed.

Retrieving the bow from Anna, "It's supposed to be taut, aye," Hilda replied as she lifted the bow, sighted it in the direction of intention and loosed the oak stave nocked to her weapon. The arrow struck true into the intended target. Bringing her bow down to her side, she peered out the corner of her eye towards Anna. "An' if we live through this, I'll teach ye how to string it," she chided with a warm smile.

They stood on something similiar to an archery range, cobbled together with little more than creativity and necessity atop the hill, at the edge of the upper camp. Flanked by ancient trees, this space provided a modest space for the rebels to practice their archery away from the main campfires. Felled branches and fallen logs served as makeshift targets, scattered at varying distances. The rebels who gathered here did not come to hone a skill for sport. They were preparing in the name of the cause. In Anna's case, her preparation of strength, skill and instruction from a new found friend helped give her hope to face the looming threat der Flechtemann now invited to their door.

Hilda, her weathered face flashing a mischievious grin, stood beside Anna, who looked distinctly bemused. The sparse sunlight filtered through the foliage above, casting dappled shadows on uneven ground.

"Right, well, I've never done any shootin', not with a proper bow. Slings and the like, aye, my best weapons, even a flimsy bow good fer huntin' rabbit, but the draw on this is somethin' else," Anna admitted, stretching her sore arm.

"Come on, yer no maiden. I've seen ye carry pots would snap a man's back in twain, aye," Hilda chuckled, watching Anna's face grimace at new found muscle pains. "Me uncle doesna' much know 'ow much shootin' I done, or he'd be at me heels. I wanted t'learn bladework when I be a little'un, but this be better, thinks I. A blade be fine, but a'times ye need to keep distance. That be where the bow makes 'erself known." She paused with a glance to Anna. "Ye'll get the hang o'it in time."

"Right," Anna said. "It's why I be wantin' to learn it."

"Then watch and learn, lass," Hilda kidded, her eyes narrowing at the target down range. With a fluid motion, she pulled back and released the arrow. The shaft struck the branch with satisfying precision, the sharpened point burrowing deep into the targeted branch thirty paces away.

Anna's eyes widened, a mix of awe and determination in her gaze. "Yer a miracle. To help yer father, Werner, with the healin' arts, and then to understand marshal skills. Teach me what ye can. I be willin'."

Hilda grinned with the willingness to become the teacher. Once again handing the bow to Anna, she assured, "I'm no' as good as yer Da, but it took even me time. Yer not goin' to get so good in so short a time—but I can teach ye t'shoot straight an' well."

"It'll do, aye," Anna conceded.

"Right then, again, get yerself the feel o' the bow." Hilda held the bow out to Anna, this time taking more time to explain. Anna grasped the bow in the way Hilda demonstrated, "Ye Hold it steady. Raise yer bow hand to eye level and draw the string with three fingers 'till it touch the tip of your nose and lower lip. Yer fingers and nocked arrow needs rest jus' below yer chin. Shootin' the likes o'this bow be all about control."

Over the next hour, Hilda guided Anna through the basics of archery. She showed her how to properly nock an arrow, adjust her grip on the bow, and draw the string. Anna struggled initially, the bowstring biting into her fingers, but with each attempt, she grew more comfortable. Fallen leaves crunched beneath their boots while the distant murmur of the rebel camp's activity provided a distant backdrop for their natural classroom.

As they practiced, Hilda's calloused and weathered hands moved with a fluidity that came from countless hours of practice. Anna, in contrast, still unaccustomed to the bow in hand, her posture uncertain, did her best to mimick Hilda's movements. The bow string taut in her grip as she struggled to draw the bow and replicate the seasoned mentor's grace. Every once in a while, Hilda adjusted Anna's stance to help align her to the target. So far, Anna hit nothing—though her errors were at least growing less numerous.

"There y'go, lass. Yer getting' the hang o' it," Hilda encouraged, observing Anna's progress.

As the sun dipped below the horizon, casting long shadows over the crude archery pitch, Anna finally managed to hit a target. The arrow struck the edge of a branch, careening into the larger trunk below, twanging from its own momentum. There it lodged firmly without falling to the ground.

Hilda clapped Anna on the back, her approval evident. "No' bad, Anna! Excellent strength in your draw and aim. Put some time in, and ye shall be puttin' them where ye want. But tell me, why now?"

"Sieg and Dieter, they didna' want me fightin',"Anna hesitated, her eyes flickering with a hint of moisture, now looking at Hilda's curved smile. "But there be a fight comin', and I need t'help wi' the rest o'ye somehow.

"Why me help do ye need?" Hilda raised a brow. "An' why the secrecy, from yer kin?"

"Ye nay ken me meanin, Sieg doesna' want me t'fight in the first place—and I donna' want Dieter seeing me with a bow." She paused, drawing up her height, "I donna' want 'im to fight neither even though I know he be a man wi' his own pride, but..."

167

But I may have already lost a brother, she thought, then tried to push the despairing thought away.

Hilda's expression softened, a silent understanding passing between them. "I ken what ye be meanin'. But in these times, everyone needs to chip in. Besides…" She paused looking at Anna from her slightly cocked head and smiled with a wrinkle of her nose, "He be nay so young in willin' spirit and stunnin' strength as ye place on him."

Anna nodded reluctantly, a question forming in her mind. *Was the whole reason she joined the rebels t'keep him safe.* She wondered. "I just want to protect him."

Hilda's gaze lingered on Anna, a flicker of empathy in her eyes. "We all want to protect someone. That be why we fight. But remember, lass, it's not jus' 'bout the ones close to ye. 'Tis about *all* of us. We stand together, see? Ye may consider ye might be a bit more protective than need be." She finished the statement with a broad smile.

Anna nodded, but said nothing. She felt hypocritical, with her conflicting loyalties to the camp and to her brother. Now, too, she sensed something else in Hilda about her brother, a strange quick glance up the trail to the camp appeared to signal a deeper thinking.

"Hilda?" she asked refocusing the conversation. "When did ye learn to shoot a bow?"

Hilda's toughened fingers tightened around the bow, a distant look in her eyes. Anna's question cut through the present moment chasing the reverie of the moment away. Wisps of blond hair, freed from her braids, fluttered in the wind as she picked up the recollection of a time past.

"It was a…a bad time, Anna," she replied, her voice carrying a mixture of resignation and guarded vulnerability.

168

"Y'learn things when ye've got nay choice. A bit like yer learnin' now, see."

Anna sensed a reluctance in Hilda's response. An unspoken weight hung in the air. She decided not to press further, recognizing the ache of emotion in Hilda's eyes, an ache seen before by Anna in the eyes of many women. She saw the look when she was a child, first in her own mother's eyes, and then among the rare guests they received before Karl went fully into the bottle—neighboring men whose wives with exhausted eyes seemed to say, *I have a wound that I cannot heal.* Forcing Hilda to dredge up old hurts was not an intention Anna wished to pursue.

As the archery session drew to a close, Hilda observed Anna's progress with quiet satisfaction. Another thud of an arrow hitting its makeshift target echoed through the clearing, and a sense of accomplishment settled between the two women. Anna lowered the bow, wincing at the sore muscles of her back.

Hilda clapped a hand on Anna's shoulder, smiling. "Y'did well."

Anna returned the smile, gratitude shining in her eyes. "With yer help, aye."

As they made their way back to the heart of the camp, Anna noticed a figure in the distance. There, her father, der Flechtemann stood, his gaze fixed on the archery range. Lines etched into his weathered face betrayed no emotion, but his eyes held a silent acknowledgment of satisfaction. Anna met his gaze, uncertainty yet defiance flickered in her eyes. Unpredictably, her father said nothing to stop her, and for some unforeseen reason, in her mind, she did not expect a caution from him.

As they passed, Hilda offered a subtle nod to der Flechtemann, a silent exchange of understanding. Anna, catching the unspoken language between the two rebels, suddenly realized what was meant. Her father was responsible for Hilda's encouragement to train on the bow.

Did he know I would ask her? She wondered. *Did he ask her to help me?* Somehow, she thought this reasonable. Despite herself, a bit embarrassed, a new found sense of connection with her father, a bridge being forged in a shared purpose, began to emerge… *or maybe not* she thought?

Der Flechtemann's gruff voice broke the stillness. "We'll need e'ery hand."

Anna hesitated, then nodded. As she passed him by, she looked askew towards him, she noticed the warmth in his eye—and though she tried to retain her anger for him, a part of her continued to soften.

***

As he watched his daughter pass him by, Hans Symon retreated back into the famliliar folds of der Flechtemann. The cares and worries of a father subsided, replaced by one of the finest tactical minds in this mockery of an Empire—a sham, far from both holy or Roman, held up by the arbitrary beureaucratic bulk of countless landowners, monks, moneylenders, merchants, and clerks.

Now, from the vantage point atop the hillock, the old rebel surveyed the makeshift "advance camp" sprawling beneath him like a cluster of haphazardly arranged game pieces. The sparks of new, misleading fires whispered their smoke into the night sky, and the low murmur of hushed conversations and the occasional clink of chainmail, adjusted by the wearer, echoed through the shadows.

His beard grown grey and the loss of more friends than he wanted to remember brought on a very lonesome existence. Years of hit and run warfare for the cause of freedom, now began to take its toll on his bearing. The shadow of Hans Symon caught up with der Flechtemann, during perhaps the most concentrated reprisal efforts ever garnered by him from his enemies. His band of patriots, pursued as common criminals by hirelings of a corrupt Abbot through frost and plague, his son, Yakov, lost to a brilliant plan devised by ruthless mercenaries wore deep into his aging warrior's psyche. And now, an imminent attack, orchestrated by the Chain and his band of sellwords loomed like a dark storm on the horizon.

How came this? He wondered.

That very question haunted der Flechtemann as he reflected on years of resistance, the clandestine maneuvers, and the calculated strikes against the priests and the petty kings, the princes and the sellwords, the preachers and the corrupt merchants who constantly exploited the common folk. And now, the Abbot's gold flowed freely through Helmstedt and Schoningen, right into the pockets of the jackal knight named Petres, a sellword himself. The Chain served the one who paid him the most, and such was the way of the scoundrel.

At the thought of the mercenary, the lines etched on his weathered face deepened. Der Flechtemann baited this trap, and prepared as well as he could for every possible eventuality. Yet even now, his mind raced, considering a carefully crafted counterplan—his chief concern… what if the Chain did not play his game? His training of his leaders

171

would have to suffice. They would have to pivot quickly, turning the change into their favor.

"If he doesn't attack," Der Flechtemann muttered to himself. His hands clenched into fists, calloused from years of wielding weapons and orchestrating covert operations. The mere thought of uncertainty gnawed at him, for in years past he honed his plans into certainties—and as well planned as his strategy now seemed, even the smallest margin of error chafed at him.

He would not worry so if his son, Yakov, was not a pawn in this dangerous game. This plan hinged on Petres' ruthlessness, on the assumption the Chain would seize the opportunity to strike the heart of the rebellion, seeking retribution for the raids and humiliations suffered at the rebels' hands.

Yet, what if Petres hesitated? What if the mercenary leader perceived the trap, or worse, if he decided to alter the course of his journey to this Toranj, this stronghold, with Yakov still in tow? The old rebel's jaw clenched, frustration and fear intertwining like serpents in the pit of his stomach. Below, oblivious to the internal turmoil of their leader, the rebels continued their preparations, guided by the belief their cause was just and their leader's foresight would lead them to victory.

"Ho, leader o' the cause," came an unfittingly cheerful voice. Der Flechtemann half-turned to see Nerijus. Smiling, the rebel walked over, wearing mail and carrying an ax and a strangely oval wooden shield painted with a design der Flechtemann did not recognize—interlocking and overlapping red lines meant little to him.

172

"The cause be the leader. I be only the first among followers," der Flechtemann replied, gesturing at the shield. "The device 'pon yer shield is new?"

Nerijus shrugged. "Fer us, it stands fer life an' death—an' how everythin' connects. We wear it t'honor our fallen. I wear it fer every good rebel we've lost to yon hounds who be advancin' now."

Der Flechtemann nodded. He could almost feel the weight of the many men and women who died defending this cause. For a moment, staring into the space above his scout's head, he fancied he could see those warriors of the past stretching out in long rows behind Nerijus.

"Ye look lost," Nerijus observed. "All be well?"

Shaking his head the reverie stepped aside. "Hm," der Flechtemann grunted. In the distance, he could see Sieg and Dieter climbing back up to the main camp—and not too far, der Flechtemann knew Elias would be kneeling in prayer in his tent.

"Yer handlin' the defence," der Flechtemann commanded.

"Aye! I will," Nerijus nodded, surprised. "I thought ye would look to one o' the others."

"They be me bow an' spear," der Flechtemann said, clapping Nerijus on the shoulder with firm affirmation. "And ye are me shield. I charge ye with defending this hill whilst I do as I must."

Nerijus nodded, before hesitating, posing a question. "I know ye has a plan—but what be the extent of it? Ye shall ride with Elias and Sieghart, but where to?"

173

"Where I ought t'have gone far sooner," der Flechtemann said, a sad tinge in his voice, but with calm assurance, as he walked away. "To protect me child."

Chapter XIV: Battle of the Hill

"I fear the fickle, for I fear the tree without roots; I fear lest it fall with a gust…[And] man was born anchored to his mother; and till he dies, he must have an anchor, something to believe…a God to know, or a cause to love. [For what] good is struggle without a hill to call home?"

-Brother Jakob, circa 1384

Dawn cracked the sky with a cold, cloudy light, by the sun diffused in a dirty yellow glow. Petres the Chain sat mounted atop his steed, his mercenary forces assembled behind him. They arrived having marched on a trail deep in muck and mire of wet forest and tall grass, forced to spend two nights in the cold, early wintery chill. Now, they faced the wooded hill, with the rebel camp sprawled below in sparse disarray, an entrance to hell guarded by the desperate and defiant.

Mercenaries, sellword's all, now assembled for war, positioned in the center of the force, stood grim-faced in uneven ranks, their attire a patchwork of worn gambesons, chainmail hauberks, and the occasional mismatched piece of plate armor scavenged from fallen foes. A few wore coifs beneath their helmets, the chainmail providing a meager defense against the relentless barrage of black-tufted arrows that often marked their engagements. Spears, maces, and axes stood tall in the hands of the men, well-kept for a mercenary outfit. The stench of sweat and oiled-metal hung

175

in the air, blending with the damp, cold smell of the forest floor.

Left and right of the mass assembled in the meadows near the foot of the partisan defenses, trained infantrymen carried shields and wore fitted, open-faced armets over their coifs. Gambesons, worn over chainmail, offered an additional layer of protection. The once-vibrant colors of the padded garments had faded to a dull palette, blending with the hardened expressions etched into the faces of the men beneath.

To this, archer's sporting kettle hats, bows held at ease in one hand, a quiver of arrows across their backs, their uniform gambesons worn with pride, arranged themselves in ranks to the rear of the mercenary and infantry formations.

The Chain's small cavalry of knights seeking favor of their masters or the Abbot and their retainers ranged the ground just behind the archers waiting to pounce whichever direction their leader felt the need to strengthen the attack.

Petres the Chain remained at the fore of this grim congregation, riding back and forth on his spirited Andalusian mount, an inky silhouette against the cloudy sky. His new armor, missing gauntlets, and tassets, yet gifted to him by the Abbott during his respite in Helmstedt, created a threatening visage on the field of battle. Today would be a fitting day for the first wearing of such an indulgence.

He stopped near the center of the force where his second in command, Dumas, and five of his lieutenants held parley. Lifting his helm from his head he placed it in the crook of his arm. His proud mount nervously bobbed its head in anticipation, which brought the Chain's gentling hand to pat the horse's neck. The view of the field of battle now more clearly in his sight, a smile played on his face. A cruel scar received in a battle long ago, produced a deep shadow across his cheek like some twisted badge of honor.

Standing in his stirrups, Petres surveyed the rebel camp laid out at the base of a steep rise on the far side of the meadow just out of arrow shot. Worries now cast assuredly aside brought his focus to the task before him. There would be a reckoning today, for on this day he would extract a nagging thorn from his side and bring the rebel der Flechtemann and his ilk to complete defeat. His force of nearly eight hundred, some being new to the force having joined as indentured to some of the landed lords along the way, to his assurance, would easily carry the day.

His second, Dumas, sat his mount at attention, as stoic as ever, a bit more presumptuous than his leader would like. The Chain's smile slipped by a smidge as he looked at him. Petres' leutenants noting the leaders' slight, moved aside. The scarred mercenary, driven by a volatile mix of pride and fury, turned his horse to cast a shadow on Dumas as he addressed his men.

"Look at 'em," Petres sneered, his voice carrying the weight of gravel and malice. "Thought they could slip away into the night, hide in them mountains like rats. But we found 'em, lads! We dragged 'em from the shadows, and now they be cowerin' at the foot o' this damn hill, thinkin' their defense against a'for a high bank be in their favor." His men listened in silence. Some adjusted their weapons, others flexed their scarred knuckles, all awaiting his command.

Petres continued, his laughter, like punctuation for emphasis, echoed through the still dawn air. "Ah, they be thinkin' they're safe down here, cowerin' behind battlements at the base of a hill! They think they can keep eatin' away at our peace, raidin' like sea-dogs, while we sit in place. Well, we be nay fools! And we're 'ere t'burn this camp, rebels and all. Ain't no sanctuary fer the damned."

As a dark echo of assent spread through the men, Petres turned to Dumas, his eyes piercing through the stoic facade. He grinned madly addressing his appointed captain.

"O, Dumas, this be a happy day!" he said, almost singsong. "My brave, trusted second, this rot confronting us be yer doin', and ye win every accolade fer the victory we shall have. Ye wanted this, aye? Ye came t'me with news o' brewin' mutiny in the ranks, like a good, honest man, an' I *never* forget a face. Yer impatience and second guessing ha' won the prize. Ye want the rewards o' leadership. So good luck to ye, Dumas."

Dumas sat still, growing pale. "Fer what, sire?"

"Oh, fer leadin' us against these dogs! See, I give thee a privilege, and it be that o' leadin' the initial charge. Show 'em, good man, *what it means t'cross the Chain.*" Petres' retorted in his angered growl.

He spat these last words with a sickening smile, his hand at his hilt, and Dumas could only nod. To lead the first assault against a camp full of archers was a death sentence, and they both knew it.

"'Fit be yer will," Dumas managed, his mouth dry.

"Oh nay," the Chain admonished. "Say nay that. This be yer own will, now fulfilled. Rejoice, Dumas. Give me a smile."

With a sickly, pallid smile, Dumas accepted the unclear honor bestowed upon him. There was no option now, he knew. The Chain regarded the temper of the will of the men and made his decision. They would not mutiny against

178

him, certainly not for a single man's sake. Though being the thinker he was, the Chain felt the lesson would suffice to win the refocus of the army at hand. With Dumas in a precarious position, possibly doomed to oblivion, he would again restore order and be able to destroy his sworn enemy in der Flechtemann. As Petres lay his war hammer on Dumas's shoulder like a king knighting an honored servant, the tension between the two figures simmered momentarily, the clash of wills only masked by the intended façade of unity.

"God go with ye, friend Dumas," Petres said with understated benevolence, glancing to the men gathered nearest him. "Dumas, the bravest of ye, shall lead ye in the first assault! Remember, a corpse fer every arrow!"

The mercenaries, hungry for blood, vengeance, and glory, roared in approval, spittle flying from their mouths. Dumas looked at them inanely, remembering only a few days ago, they rode on the edge of mutiny… whispers carried on most men's lips… until Dumas's warning led them to this dubious result… possibly to his own doom. *I should have let them cut his heart out,* Dumas bitterly thought, even as he nodded at their applause and raised his axe.

Now, Petres watched with dark satisfaction as Dumas led the vanguard toward the open field before them, each step bringing them closer to the rebel camp. Petres, left commanding the rest of the army, gazed at the hill with a calculating glint in his eye. He knew this was a trap, some clever snare laid by the rebels—but like the name he bore, he was chained to the will of his men. The scar, the humiliation, the simmering mutiny among the mercenaries—all came together to play a part in the assault laid before him, for better or worse.

179

"Oh, but I will win," he muttered, drawing in a long breath as he kissed the head of his war hammer. "Saints gran' me strength, if any of ye still ha' ears t'listen. Give me yon bastard's head, an' I shall bedeck thy chapels with indulgences."

As the first light of dawn cast long shadows across the battleground-to-be, Petres took a final, lingering glance at the pitiful camp at the foot the hill. How few rebels were left—*soon, there may be none at all*, he surmised. The proverbial thorn in his side may finally be removed. Smiling at the thought despite his misgivings, the mercenary leader braced himself for what awaited, the discordant clash of metal, the screams of the wounded, and another butchery well-done.

***

.

The rebel camp was alive with a chaotic hum of preparation. Anna, her blonde hair partially concealed by the hood of her cloak, walked alongside Hilda, nervously checking her bow.

"'Tis strung rightly?" she asked for the third time.

Hilda smiled wryly. "Oh saints, yer a bundle o' nerves. Shoulda at' some o' yer own stew. That set my stomach right."

"I could nay eat like this," Anna muttered. "This wait be keepin' me in anguish of what may come."

Just then, Anna stopped in her tracks. Dieter, clad in a new gambeson and carrying a spear and shield which appeared to outsize him, coming across unwieldy in his

180

hands, moved through makeshift pathways between tents, jaw set, eyes focused on the line he meant to join.

"No," she breathed, and before Hilda could stop her, she quickened her pace to catch up with him. She reached out, her fingers closing around his forearm with a force that matched the frustration simmering within her.

"Oi, wait," she said angrily, her green eyes flashing with exasperation. "What does ye think yer doin'?"

Dieter slowed but didn't turn to face her. "Anna, we donna' got time for it. I've got me duty."

Anna tightened her grip, frustration boiling over. "Yer a fool, Dieter. Who got ye that spear? If it be Sieg, I swear I'll—"

He finally turned to face her, his dark eyes widening as he saw Anna, her blonde hair framing a face flushed with concern, clutched a bow in her hands—a visible sign of her newfound role in the rebellion.

"You what?" Dieter said, startled. Angrily, he pulled out of her grasp. "Are ye mad?"

"As mad as ye," Anna muttered, before arguing. "Come off it. Lay down that spear, an' then we'll—"

"We'll what?" Dieter shot back, his voice edged with frustration. "Gah, this rebellion, it be gettin' out o' hand! I be old enough to make this decision meself. Ye canna' keep protectin' yer little brother, as I be." He paused looking Anna directly, "And, I can't let ye throw yerself into this mess alone!"

Just then Nerijus, with his shield slung across his back, approached them, sensing the rising tension. "Now, now, ye stubborn twain," he said in his mild tone. "Does nay

181

ye know we be needin' every hand we can get? It be nay time fer family squabbles, entertainin' though they be ta'e the likes o'those around," he affirmed looking over his shoulder at other partisans gathered close by.

Anna turned to Nerijus, glaring. "Ye stay out o' it. He be my little brother. I canna' bear the thought o' him getting' hurt…he can't."

Dieter shot Nerijus a defiant look. "An' I won't stand by and watch me own sister go out shootin' twigs at hungry jackals!"

"Look, either y'both fight, or none o' ye do. So does ye both agree to withdraw?" Nerijus quarried, the argument placated for the moment. Neither nodded. He clapped his hands. "All be well, then! Anna, ye'll be position'd at the edge with yer nice new bow. An' Dieter, y'proud new warrior, ye'll be part o' my shield wall. See? We need both o' ye, and we need thee t'be focused on the task at hand."

"But—" Anna began, only to be cut off by Nerijus's unusually firm gaze.

"Nay 'buts' from ye, either o' ye! We're in this together, aye? We canna' afford nay discord when the real fightin' begins. So say aye, or get goin' t'the rear."

Anna and Dieter exchanged a glance, a reluctant agreement passing between them. They both knew Nerijus was right—no room could be tolerated for disputes in the face of a common threat. Their shoulders slumping with resignation, the siblings took a collective breath

In unintended unison the "aye" came. Nerijus grinned.

As the tension eased, Nerijus continued, "Right now. Ye each ha' yer own path in this rebellion. Accep' that, an' focus on what need be doin'. Now, get yerselves ready, ye greenhorns! Them bastardin' sellswords won't wait fer disagreements!"

They nodded, acknowledging the order as they turned away. Through the muted sounds of sharpening blades and the distant hum of preparations, Anna and Dieter descended the hillside together, their footsteps silent in the cold, wet grass. The cloudy light of the overcast day cast a somber hue over them as they moved toward the false camp at the foot of the hill.

"Keep yerself low," Dieter asserted as they skulked through the trees. "Won't do t'have the enemy see us descendin' the hill, or the plan's gone t'hell."

Anna nodded, then stole a sidelong glance at her brother. His broad shoulders and sullen demeanor a stark contrast to the wide-eyed child she once knew. "Dieter," she began, breaking the heavy silence between them as they walked, "I be sorry. Ye are a stout brother o'mine, and I can honor that in ye; however, this isn't what I imagined fer us."

Dieter grunted in acknowledgment, his gaze fixed on the path ahead. "Imagine so—but I be seein' now life rare turns out as ye or I may imagine, Anna. Ye were always lookin' out fer me, but it went the other way around as well— I never wanted t'see ye wieldin' a bow like that father o' ours."

Anna sighed, her fingers absently playing with the unfamiliar weapon in her hands. "Things...*change*." She said moving on with further thought. "Folk change. An' this rebellion, it be not just 'bout us. It be about everyone who be sufferin' under the rule of those in power."

183

Dieter's grip tightened on his spear, the worn wood a tangible connection to the harsh reality of their situation. "Ye always were a believer, sister. I understand it—but it don't be meanin' I have to *like* it. I get the feelin' we're marching to our doom, and I don't be meanin' this battle, Anna. I mean *this rebellion*."

Anna glanced at him disapprovingly. "Well, we can't jus' stand by. The rebels we stand beside, they be fightin' fer something greater, and it be only right we be a part of it. And if ye nay be a believer, why be ye here? Why be ye luggin' about a spear an' makin' fer battle?"

"Fer family," Dieter said quietly. "Fer a sister who believes too much, an' a brother who only believed tha' he believes."

Anna fell quiet, then. The path leveled out as they approached the false camp, the makeshift defenses becoming more apparent. The clever ruse, designed to divert the attention of the impending mercenaries, now grew more convincing. The bushels of hay, the tents, they all made it seem like a proper enough camp.

Hilda and a line of archers to one side of the camp signaled for Anna's attention. She paused and waved back. Half turning to her brother in parting, "Well, I best be with the others," now suddenly reluctant to leave him alone. "Ye know the plan, aye? We're t'retreat—"

"I know," Dieter said, then grunted a disapproving rasp. "Nerijus be right… I s'pose. We all have our paths. Jus' wish ours did nay lead us into such a mess a' this."

Anna turned full to face Dieter and placed her practiced hand on her brother's shoulder. "Look ye at me, Dieter. We'll be gettin' through this, ye and I both, aye?... Together…We always have."

Nerijus, approached Anna and Dieter and pausing briefly to watch the two siblings hug. He smiled at them warmly. "So ye made up—that be good! I admire ye both fer yer hearts. But now be time to brace yerselves. The storm's 'bout to strike." Nerijus paused looking beyond the false camp, then continued, "May our camp be an ark in the flood," he prayed.

Dieter nodded uncertainly as the rebel moved on. "Strange man," he muttered,

"Dieter, look ye at me," Anna said. He complied, seeing the worry and pride in her eyes. "Ye promise me ye'll stay safe," she whispered.

Dieter nodded. "And ye as well."

In a rare moment of vulnerability, they embraced one last time. The hug brief but meaningful lasting long enough for both to pray in their hearts the other would survive this battle.

Then a horn sounded, and they looked up to see Nerijus approaching, axe raised. "Enemy on th'march!" he called. "Off to yer stations all. Stragglers, plug the shield wall!"

The siblings nodded and ran to their posts. As Anna hurriedly asked Hilda to check the stringing of her bow yet again, Dieter gulped as he found himself shoulder to shoulder with two rebels. Today he would fight not only for the cause and his sister and brother, but for the person to his right and to his left, standing ground united against a common enemy. Suddenly, the weather seemed warm, almost hot—more likely the sweat and heat of their trepidation. He recognized the men on either side of him. One a scrawny, bright-eyed man named Bertolf, and the other an older man named Marttinen. The latter man's lip

185

quivered. Dieter could hear him mumbling in a language he did not know.

"Raise yer shields, form the wall… plug the gaps!" came Nerijus' command.

Bile began to rise in his stomach. *They must be near,* Deiter tought. Feeling sick, suddenly he wretched on the ground in front of him, covering his feet with slimy mucus. Embarrased he quickly returned erect, his shield plugging the gap in the wall before him.

The older man, Marttinen, to one side of Dieter smiled and simply said, "'appens to we all a'times."

Almost on cue, the clank and shudder of a marching army came upon their ears. Behind them, a horn blared. From a low ridge slightly behind the advance camp, Anna exhaled as she released an arrow alongside the rest of the archers. Momentarily transfixed by the arc of the soaring projectile, she almost forgot to shoot again, until Hilda elbowed her.

"Don't look at 'em!" Hilda hissed. "No time! Keep releasin' unto the mass!"

Anna nodded, nocking another arrow to her bow. The marching formation of mercenaries seemed to flinch from their first volley, but the next did not phase them. Their pace, instead, seemed to quicken.

Below, Dieter could see them now, almost deafened by the clank of armor and the stamp of boots as the mercenaries closed in on the false camp. Dieter raised his shield, his hands grasping the worn wooden grip with a white-knuckled intensity. Beside him, Bertolf adjusted his speckled, thin frame, while Marttinen continued to mumble under his breath.

As the mercenaries approached, the sickening realization continued to broil in Dieter's stomach. No mere skirmish advanced before the assembled rebels. The approaching force, formidable in scope, promised to be a true clash of blood and chaos. Somewhere in the back of his mind he knew it would be so, yes,—but to see it now brought on an entirely different picture of scale reinforcing new fear.

I could die, Dieter thought reverberating from deep within his inner core, as if the warning wafted to him on a whim over a great distance. *I could die today.*

Perched on the ridge above the shield wall, Anna feared for her brother. She could see him from here. Thankfully, he was only at the flank of their defense, some distance from the bulking weight of the enemy's central assault.

"Archers, hold!" came Nerijus's command. Anna felt herself grow cold as the line of mercenaries advanced. Hilda said to her she would be required to shoot coordinated volleys, depending on command—but Anna's fingers itched to shoot now, trying to stem the tide of the Chain's men, to save the shield wall and Dieter somehow reducing the force of the attack.

"Loose!" Nerijus finally roared.

Anna pulled back her bow. She and the archers let go a coordinated volley of arrows, the sky now a cloud of the deadly flight. She could see indistinct forms of the mercenaries crumpling under the onslaught, but too few. Others filled the gaps instantly, in what seemed to her like a relentless tide of armor and malice.

The mercenaries were nearly upon the rebel defenders. Dieter, in the formation to first confront the attack, could feel the tension rise. The enemy so close now,

187

he could see the very whites of the eyes. The thrum of charging feet and the sound of clanking armor, plus the war cry of the attacker on the breeze electrified the field of battle, permeating with the crackling of fear and anticipation.

"Steady, lads!" Nerijus bellowed, his axe gleaming in the dull light. "This is where we make 'em bleed fer e'ery inch o' ground!"

Dieter's grip on his shield tightened, as the collision came—a thunderous clash of steel against wood and leather.

Having survived first contact with the Chain's army, Dieter now became very aware what he faced was perhaps the weak part of the enemy formation. The motly sellsword bulk of the opposing army struck the center of the rebel line of shields. Though feeling the pressure on the flank from the sellswords' center as he did, Dieter soon found himself confronted with well-prepared troops of the Chain's regulars begin to turn of the flanks of the partisans.

The plan for deception by the rebels, for a moment, seemed very far away. The shield wall held, but as Dieter defended himself from the first swing of an enemy axe, the force of the impact on his raised shield immediately numbed his arm. Reacting then out of fear more than skill, Dieter screamed and jabbed with his own short spear, the tip of the blade finding a mark and biting into the open thigh of a mercenary. The man screeched with pain as the din of battle increased. The merc's head now thrown back presented an easy target. Dieter, recovering from the blow saw Bertolf's spear flash, sinking into the combatant's throat. Dieter looked quickly to the rebel at his side, giving a slight nod, then immediately reacting to another blow, found himself embroiled once again in the fray.

"Look in front!" Caught in the moment, Bertolf frantically said. "Keep fightin', lad!"

And as Dieter did just that, his arms felt heavy. Up on the ridge, as Anna numbly shot arrow after arrow, the first advance of the mercenary army seemed to be slowing. She could see corpses laying on the field below, blossoms of red growing in the snow, Anna felt a pit in the bottom of her stomach.

In the quieting aftermath of this first contact, Anna recollected Yakov's demeanor toward Petres the Chain and his inclusion as a once mercenary in the Chain's battles. *Is this what you saw, Yakov?* She shuttered in thought.

"Begin retreat!" bellowed Nerijus at the top of his lungs, the words punctuated by a blowing horn. Slowly, carefully, the rebels began to pull back, archers first, then the infantry, step by step, with the center of the line folding in as the mercenary push seemingly drove a wedge into them. As Nerijus gritted his teeth from his vantage point, he waited for the line to break. Down below, Dieter took steps back on shaking legs, hackles raised on the back of his neck as enemy spears jabbed and struck at his shield, which seemed to feel far more flimsy than usual, though he knew the protection would do. His arm hurt from the effort, and he jabbed over the top of the shield occasionally, a half-hearted attempt to relieve the strain on his numb arm.

With the sudden tide of change, battles often displayed, the center of the rebel line disintegrated as the mercenary wedge drove through. The mercenary commander on horse led his men into the breech— a pale, bald man, tall and brutish, encouraged the mercenary guard onward. Though, it was not the Chain himself who led. The commander of the charging army now found himself flanked on two sides by the partisan band. Fear etched deep lines in

189

the corners of his mouth and eyes as he recognized, albeit
to late, what was about to take place. The trap now set by the
rebels, lured the unknowing mercenaries to follow in the
ruse.

"Clear!" Nerijus roared.

Immediately, the broken center of the rebel infantry
folded back from the melee, now circling back up the sides
of the rough hill to flank the enemy in a pincher movement.
The startle mercenaries, unaware of the danger as their
fanaticism followed their charging commander, attempted to
give chase, but being used to fighting in open and somewhat
level ground, or in the streets of vilages and cities, were
unused to the rough, wet terrain. They slipped and skidded
as they attempted to give chase up the incline. The
commander of the mercenaries realizing the trap before him,
stood in his saddle, screaming, "*Hold!* Give no chase, ye
fools. *Hold yer line!*"

But it was too late.

Over the din of battle a horn sounded from the rebel
cause followed by a command, which came from Nerijus as
he roared, "Send 'em to hell!" On queue from the horn the
archers turned and loosed a volley of arrows into the center
of the mercenary ranks thus covering the retreat of the
partisans foot soldiers. Within only a brief moment the rebel
contingent of soldiers turned too, to squeeze in on the enemy
trapped in the middle of the slope of the hill.

From up above, on the hill, the rear guard of rebels,
women, older men, and children, released a delicate balance
of branches, which held back a mass of large stones and logs.
As Dieter watched in horror, the mass of rolling logs and
rumbling stones fell over the side of the hill, smashing head-
long into the mercenary wedge, who, seeing the threat,

attempted a retreat. In the ensuing chaos armor and flesh split under rocks, logs smashed through ribs and broke limbs. The yells of a charging mercenary army soon turned into the anguish of the injured and last echoing voice of the dying.

Anna gasped as she saw the devastation that fell upon the enemy. Those survivors of the Chain's army which could walk or run retreated dragging as many of their fellow injured peers as they could reasonably carry; however, too, fearful of being still in arrowshot of the wooded fortress, afore unseen on the top of the hill. Mercifully, Nerijus gave no such command, and the bleeding, maimed mercenaries were allowed to retreat.

"Should'a shot em," Hilda muttered, then smirked darkly at Anna's incredulous expression marking the emotion of this unassuming young woman of mercy. "Oh, ye think me a harpy. But mark me words—they'd have nay shown us any such mercy."

"We be nay them," Anna muttered—but as she saw the mass of the dead, a worm of uncertainty crept over her.

***

"I knew it," Petres hissed as he cantered forward with his honor guard of mounted mercenaries. "I knew they had a damned trick. Another damned trick! I tire so of these gnats, may the 'eavenly father gut them all! But nay, he does nothing I say…"

Still mumbling to himself, he met the retreating advance force in whose charge, Dumas, his second in

191

command, led. Reports from the battle identified the ruse laid out perfectly by the rebels. Presenting a soft belly center of the line, the mercenaries found themselves drawn in. Out flanked by the rebel army, the mercenaries were left fighting for their very lives as their phalanx shattered. To this, at the fore of the battlefield, another defensive position set by the rebels unleashed smashing terror among the ranks. The only avenue left for the Chain's defeated men was to retreat the way in which they came. Wholly shattered the survivors dragged the injured and dying back to the shelter of the main army.

Looking over the motley crew as they straggled back, he saw a man dragging Dumas, grasping him under the bald mercenary's armpits.

"Ye, let off," Petres snarled, dismounting. "Let me see yer brave leader."

As the man let Dumas lay down, Petres looked down dispassionately. The pale man's form was broken and brutalized, and little seemed left in him. Black blood spluttered from his blue lips, and Petres knew this meant his lungs were beyond healing. He knelt by his former second.

"And so ye be done," Petres said without emotion.

"Aye," Dumas rasped.

"Ye be a good warrior, I'll give ye that," the Chain conceded. "But ye had t'go, y'see."

Dumas coughed. "I did…nothing wrong…"

"Did ye see him?" Petres asked, ignoring the protest.

"…Isn't…" Dumas choked out, his eyes glassy. "…Here."

192

Petres froze in pressing thought. He knew his quarry by now—*der Flechtemann led by example. There was no reason he would not be here, directing his band. None at all—unless.*

"Blackened cross!" he snarled, spittle flying madly from his mouth. "Get me horse! Ye," he pointed to a mounted guardsmen, "get the remainin' cavalry mounted and rounded—take e'ery horse, and e'ery man who knows to ride one! That bastard!"

As the men darted about readying for the chase so as not to be the target of any further threats, Petres glared with feigned sympathy at Dumas. "He's goin' fer his cub," he muttered darkly to no one in particular. "Ye hath given me one loss already today. Ye shall nay give me another. Ye hear me, fool? *This be yer fault!*"

Dumas heard nothing—he was already dead, glassy eyes affixed on the murky heavens. Blood seeped still from his mouth as men raced past him. He was but another man in a mountain of dead, and the Chain spared him not a glance as he and his men rode back, hoping to reach the supply consort and his captive, Yakov, before der Flechtemann could. Angry now at being duped one more time, Petres knew now the battle on the hill served as a diversion from the real intention of the rebel leader…to free his son.

Chapter XV: All For Thee

"A man wiser than I did such great things; he made great things; he left great things behind…and I looked from below at his works in awe. I was nothing more than the nothing I am today…and I was ashamed at being nothing. I wished I was he—I wished I could know how he became who he was.

And I asked him how he became—and I remember he smiled, and his eyes said to me, I did it all for thee…"

-Brother Jakob, circa 1384

Pain was Yakov's only companion as he swayed with the rhythmic jolts of the mercenary support supply train. Bound and battered, he could feel every bruise. The rough terrain beneath the wagon grated against his wounds, amplifying the torment that swept through his broken body.

His mind wandered among nothings. Around him, the scent of blood and dust hung heavy in the air, mingling with the tang of fear. The mercenaries he was traveling with spent most days looking at him with expressions of apathy and disdain, their eyes devoid of any shred of humanity. At this point, Yakov wondered sometimes whether their disdain for him was justified—after all, for them, he was simply a traitor for whom their fellow mercenaries died.

This line of thinking hurt his head.

The support column steadily moved towards a dire destination where the mercenaries planned to deliver Yakov for interrogation at the behest of the Chain. The very thought cut through his malnourished haze and sent a shiver through Yakov, a tremor of fear that eclipsed the physical torment.

"Toranj, they call it. a hold or keep of sorts," grumbled the older of the wagoners, startling Yakov before he realized the man was talking to his fellow driver, another mercenary.

"Right hellhole," the older man added, his voice coarse and weathered by years of rough living. He spat onto the ground.

"Aye," replied the younger driver, his eyes flickering nervously towards the horizon. "Las' folk I ran with told us they'd get us pushed in there if we made trouble for 'em."

"Trouble, eh?" The older man chuckled, a hollow sound that carried the weight of bitter experience. "More like it's where they'd send ye to rot. Many a soldier's soil'd 'imself to death in there, far fr'm honor an' glory an' the like."

The younger driver shifted uncomfortably, glancing back at Yakov, who was still staring off into nothing. The mercenary hurriedly looked back at his companion. "So…ye ever been inside?"

The older man grunted. "Once... Two months as a guard,… seemed a long time ago, though. An' I don' plan on goin' back."

"Don' wan' ta spend too long there," the younger mercenary shook his head. "Nay a likeable place, aye?"

With an indifferent nod of his head, the older driver winked at his fellow merc, spat again trying to rid himself of

195

the bitter taste the thought of Toranj left in his mouth and reined his horeses pulling the cart, not letting them lag behind the column. "Let's be getting' this over with, then. Maybe a day or two more, now—we can stay in the hamlet close by. Place smells like stale cheese and a hog's bladder, but it'll be doin' us fine fer a while."

The men returned to silence as the wagon rattled on, while Yakov's spirit wavered on the precipice of surrender.

I'm going to die in that keep, Yakov groggily surmised in the rolling stupor of days without sleep. He knew the traveling support for the Chain's army was far from Toranj, but the thought of his eminent death lay heavy on his mind. *Maybe Elias or his father would try to rescue him,* he thought. *At least he may hope so.*

Yakov's conscience, drifting in and out of exhaustion and sleep, continued his personal mental bantering. *No! That would be too dangerous for the partisans. The life of one is not worth the life of the whole. If he died in prison under the torture of the mercenary army— what then? Would Dieter or Anna ever find out? Or would they try and look for him—and what good would that do but expose them to more danger?*

Yakov tightly shut his eyes, trying to hold back every possibility of negative thought. He longed for miracles, but could not believe in them, not right now. He let out an unfathomable sigh that seemed to rise from the depths of his being. Besides, he reasoned with willing resignation, *extraordinary events just never occurred in his life.*

The sudden jolt of the wagon dropping over a rock or root in the road brought Yakov suddenly out of his stupor and back to his present predicament. A glance to his wagon driver and guard, their heads bobbing with the monotony of

196

the turning wheels and bumps in the road, showed indifference to his agony, their captive.

Where's Petres? Yakov wondered, his mind a cloud of recollection. Slowly awareness came back to him of an earlier conversation between the leader and his subordinates. Petres now led the assault on the rebel camp. The knight wanted an encounter with der Flechtemann. An encounter when delivered would put the myth of der Flechtemann to rest once and for all. Yakov recognized the madness in the Chain's demeanor bordering on fanaticism. The mercenary leader, frustrated by escape and defeat at every contact with the rebel band and their elusive leader, now determined his course. For this reason, he did not ride with the support column towards the stronghold of Toranj.

Yakov's eyes drifted to the low-hanging branches that brushed against the side of the wagon, a cruel reminder of the world outside his captivity—the air, crisp and cool, whispered of freedom denied. His mind flickered like a candle, suddenly thinking back to the homestead—to the long stretches of time spent languorously walking among the nearby groves of trees, laughing under the open sky, picking and smelling the earthy, cloying smell of mushrooms after the rains.

Despite it all, a wonderful life shined in his thoughts—it would be a shame to see it go, despite his pledge to his sister Anna and uncle Karl to return with funds to pay debts, for now, at least, he made his peace with the past.

"I be ready," he muttered to no-one.

The older mercenary looked back, puzzled. "What be ye mutterin' about, now?"

197

Without warning, a black flower sprouted from the side of the man's head, its stalk potted in pulsing red. Eyes wide amidst a shower of blood, the older man folded across the younger mercenary's lap, a black fletched arrow protruding from his skull.

"Rebels!" the younger man screamed.

Chaos erupted as the mercenaries scrambled to respond. Yakov froze—then seizing the opportunity, pain shooting through his battered body, rolled off the wagon. Landing on hands and knees, he hit the ground hard, a grimace deepening the lines in his face, his instincts kicked in, urging him to crawl away from the mayhem. Arrows whizzed through the air, finding their marks with deadly accuracy. The mercenaries, caught off guard, fumbled for their weapons, their panicked shouts blending with the sounds of battle that now surrounded them.

The younger caravan driver, reeling from the surprise attack, clutched at his weapon with white knuckles, his eyes wide in horror as a dark figure nocked a black-tufted arrow in his direction. He watched like a shocked deer as, without hesitation, the arrow found its mark. Yakov watched as the man slumped over, blood staining his garments.

Surrounding the wagons rode figures clad in cloaks, their identities concealed, moving with deadly precision. The mercenary sutlers and merc guards cowered amidst the onslaught. Yakov witnessed a familiar partially exposed face—the stoic Elias, his eyes betraying nothing as ever. He glanced at Yakov without expression, before shooting down a mercenary just as the merc grabbed Yakov's leg. Working quickly, adrenelin flowing fiercely, scrambling amidst terror and relief, Yakov kicked the dead man's hand away. Sighing in weak assurance, never sure when or where the attempt for rescue would advance, the rebels did come. Doubtless

198

somewhere in the planning, his father's wit served to counter the Chain's move in the chess match of wills once more.

"Get out of there!" Elias roared as he rode past, only feet away from Yakov's head.

Gasping to breathe, Yakov crawled away from the commotion, his limbs protesting with every movement. His heart pounding with a mixture of hope and apprehension as he sought to catch a glimpse of his rescuers.

Amidst the chaos, a familiar voice cut through the tumult. *"Yakov! Son!"*

He turned to see his father, der Flechtemann, speaking from the circling contingent of rebels. Moving toward Yakov, the rebel leader looked more gaunt than when Yakov last saw him. His beard grown more bedraggled while dark circles hung like puffy half-moons under hard, sad eyes.

Those very eyes met Yakov's, and they spoke of a terrible burden. In the same breath, der Flechtemann and his men moved with calculated efficiency to bring the mercenary support wagons to bay. Behind him, Sieghart, as broad-shouldered and graceful as Yakov remembered, swiftly dismounted, scooping Yakov off the ground.

"Saint's bones," Sieghart muttered in worry for his leader's son's appearance, his voice breaking as he felt the ribs jutting from at Yakov's side. "Yakov, what…what did they…"

"Father," Yakov croaked distantly, his voice strained from the ordeal. Sieghart looked at der Flechtemann helplessly. Seeing Yakov like this shattered Sieg's heart with sympathy for Hans, his leader.

"Keep thy spirit, me son, aye?" der Flechtemann said as he looked at Yakov's slumped form, his own voice quivering though his gaze did not waver. Yakov, exhausted by the ordeal and gratified to see his father, weakly smiled and nodded back. "We shall get thee away from here."

The rebels helped Yakov onto Sieghart's horse. In his fatigue all Yakov could feel was the warmth of friendly hands—the warmth of hard, bow-toughened hands, hands that fought and killed and suffered. They were hands of the cause. The cause which now held him upright in the saddle as Sieghart mounted, seating himself behind Yakov. The horse, a stout animal, its chestnut mane bouncing, for a moment complained at the added weight.

"There, boy," Sieghart patted it absently, before handing Yakov a cloak. "Yakov—be puttin' this on now."

Yakov complied, realizing that most of the rebels wore the same hooded cloak. What's more, each of them were backed by an extra man sitting behind him in the saddle—to act as decoys, he concluded, impressed by the notion, even in his distant state.

"We have ye," der Flechtemann said, cantering his mount beside them. He placed a hesitant hand on Yakov's head in blessing, as though wanting to say something yet unsure of what to say—but he need not have said anything at all. Yakov could see his weary, tear-wet eyes. They said enough.

"Mein Sohn," said Hans Symon smiling with relief.

"I…wondered if ye would come," Yakov rasped, a tear forming at the edge of his eye. "I…I…"

"We need leave," Elias interrupted, riding up to them with a sharp gaze as he scanned their surroundings "Aye, we've made short work o' this convoy, but I suspect there be more to—"

Out of seemingly nowhere, a horn sounded in the distance bringing all nervously alert.

***

"Dogs!" Petres the Chain snarled, spittle flying from his mouth as he charged on his great warhorse, leading a tireless cadre of mounted mercenary knights. *"Dogs! Wretched dogs!"*

The sellsword knight spurred his horse forward, a storm of fury brewing within him. The ruse at the rebels' camp, an affront to his authority, left him seething with frustration—but to realize it also a distraction, and Yakov might be lost, was too much. *That traitor was his,* he surmised—for he hoped, with a furious rage, der Flechtemann would appear here, himself.

The open plain stretched before him, an expanse of light snow covered grass that seemed to mock his pursuit. In the distance, he could see the ambushed convoy, and hints of his quarry riding away. He squinted against the sun's glare, scanning the undulating horizon where his targets were fleeing—splitting up, he realized. His frustration mounted as realization dawned upon him—the rebels, including der Flechtemann and Yakov, were all dressed alike. They seemed to wear identical cloaks, another deliberate tactic to confound him.

A guttural growl escaped his lips as he spurred his horse to greater speed, determined. His war hammer

201

bounced at his side as he gripped a great, dark lance, eager to close the distance and unleash his wrath upon the rebels. He fancied the lance as an extension of his rage—even though it was just a weapon, like any tool of war, brutish and crude, much like him.

As the chase continued, Petres felt the twinge of madness clawing at the edges of his consciousness. He needed to catch them, to make them pay for the humiliation they continually wrought upon him. The white plain over which they rode, the snow only as deep as the horse's cannon, seemed to stretch endlessly. Rivulets of sweat poured down his leathery face.

Suddenly, wicked laughter bubbled up from within the Chain. Behind him, his cadre of mercenary knights cast furtive glances at their captain, uncertain of the storm that brewed within their volatile leader.

Then, Petres' eyes narrowed upon one particular figure riding lopsided in the back saddle. A thrill surged through him, a spark of vindication. The wounded one—that was undeniably the traitorous Yakov. Under his great helm, a malevolent grin twisted Petres' scarred face. With his lance raised, he spurred his horse forward, his men fearfully trying to keep pace with the maddened leader.

As the rebels continued their flight, the unknown figure looked back, once, and it was enough—through the narrow slits of his helmet, Petres could see Yakov, his face bruised and battered, a hollow recognition in his eyes.

I come for thee, Yakov, Petres thought with bitter humor. *And I name myself thy death!*

As the distance closed, his lance aimed true, Petres the Chain prepared to bring an end to this broken rebel.

***

Yakov looked on dully as Petres gained ground.

Time did not matter right then—Yakov lived in a place without time for months now. Pain, rest, respite—everything blended, and nothing seemed to make sense. At the edge of death for so long, the approaching lance created in him a sense of relief… a euphoria of a welcome end.

Now, your watch will end, whispered a voice softly from the depths of his thoughts. *You will be free from guilt and grief for living when Mikkel does not. The rebels shall have closure, and Anna and Dieter shall have a memory to bury. Everything ends now. All will be well…*

Then, from the corner of his eye, he saw one of the rebel riders turn. A black-tufted arrow nocked and loosed before Yakov could blink. It struck the Chain's helmet, denting the metal orb as it bounced off. The mercenary's course faltered slightly—another arrow found a mark, striking the knight's horse in its buttocks. Maddened with pain, the Chain's warhorse still continued its charge—decades of breeding became evident in the animal's reaction. A third arrow found a chink in the Chain's armpit, burying itself deep within. Snarling, the Chain turned away from Yakov to glare at his new enemy…

And there, toward him, charged der Flechtemann.

Yakov watched, wide-eyed and horribly aware, as his father rode toward the lance-carrying mercenary knight. Der Flechtemann's hood was thrown back, and his wispy grey hair framed his high forehead like a ghostly halo as he charged, throwing away his bow to draw the rondel dagger at his side.

Yakov remembered that dagger—der Flechtemann had put it to his neck, the first time they met. It was not der Flechtemann holding the dagger now, but his father.

Hans Symon snarled as he rode his horse into the Chain, the mercenary's lance skewering the ribcage of the beautiful grey mount. Even as it toppled into the Chain's warhorse, Hans lept from the saddle with surprising grace, crashing into the Chain. The mercenary's helmet fell away as he twisted, his eyes wide as Hans' dagger jammed into his throat in a jet of blood, before the older man stabbed him yet again even as they toppled.

"Father!" Yakvo screamed, his voice cracking.

In a final instant, just as the horses crashed together in a mad din, his father glanced at him, eyes wet—and then, both figures collapsed into a jumble, with the horses collapsing into each other. The mercenaries on Petres' tail only barely swerved to avoid crashing into them. A few continued the chase uncertainly, while the rest milled about the sprawling mess of limbs with raised spears.

"Sieg, stop!" Yakov cried, yanking the rebel's cloak. "Halt! My father, he's—"

"I cannot," Sieghart screamed over the sound of dashing hooves. His voice quivered. "Forgive me, Yakov. He asked this o' me!"

"Nay!" Yakov croaked, begging. "Please! Please, he is important. He be yer cause! Turn back, I beg of ye…!"

"I cannot," Sieg repeated in a hoarse voice. Yakov looked back again, eyes wide. The indistinct form of the mercenaries surrounded both the Chain and his father. Nothing could be seen. No distinction could be made.

"Mein Vater," Yakov whispered. "Why? Why did ye…"

Then he remembered the look in his father's eyes.

And he knew.

Chapter XVI: Of Twilight and Dusk

"All days know dawn—but each beginning knows an end; and all days, in time, sing songs of twilight and dusk..."

-Brother Jakob, circa 1384

The forest surrounded them, its shadowy canopy providing cover for the rebels as the last traces of the red, fading sun disappeared.

Anna and Dieter trudged wearily along the trail of retreat set in motion as a necessary move to establish a new defensible position. The failed mercenary attack took its toll, but they were alive, the taste of victory bittersweet on their lips, their breath visible in the cold evening air evidence of the stress of their exertion. Anna, her new bow slung across her back, stole a glance at her brother. Dieter, even more solemn than usual, marched beside her, his eyes reflecting the grey weariness that lingered in her own.

Moving camp now became an inevitable task to keep ahead of anything the Chain might throw their way. Der Flechtemann and Nerijus knew, in time, there would need to be a final confrontation to stop Petres in his madness, but that time was not now. A defendable, protected position in continual change was the only safety the partisan army could provide. An offensive strike would come later when more to the advantage of the rebel leaders.

The rebels moved, now the forest and mercenary army left behind, in a disciplined column, led by Nerijus, whose exhausted demeanor masked by forced cheer at the slim success of the last encounter with the Chain, kept the group of patriots and their load bearing mounts moving.

The forest floor crunched beneath their boots as they walked, and around them, the fading light painted the trees in shades of gray and gold, casting long shadows across their path. The rebels, cold and worn out, left much behind in their chaotic, but well considered escape. The Chain left far too few men to sustain a siege, and the rebels

broke through the confused, wounded lines of the enemy, moving in the direction of a preplanned forest escape. Abandoned wagons and tents lay scattered back on the hill, where several mercenaries still milled about. Now, the rebels went on foot, packing what they could on the backs of surviving horses. Aside from the mounts taken by der Flechtemann's party, the rest of the horses trailed, led on tether in trains of two or three behind the rebel column, shaking their shaggy manes.

With a sigh, Nerijus called for a momentary halt. The rebels, men, women, and children, their breaths visible in the crisp air, gathered in a loose formation. Alive but in good cheer, the army of partisans found themselves riding an emotional elation heightened by their designed escape after the encounter with the mercs. Nerijus looked over the gathering noting the health of the combined army before him. Now the appearance of der Flechtemann and his guard to meet the moving column as agreed would complete the ordeal. He knew too, well laid plans often did not follow a designed unfolding, so he would move ahead and make sure this column would be safe and wait for his commander's joining.

Anna turned to Dieter, her tired green eyes reflecting the toll of the day as she hugged him. "We made it through, Dieter. 'Ere the settin' sun, we still breathe."

Dieter nodded, agreeing as she let him go, his expression, however, grave. "Aye, but at what cost? So much have we left behind. Tents and pots and pans, wagons whole, supplies such as we could nay carry—and that be tae nay mention the dead, both theirs and ours."

"T'was a battle, lad," Hilda said as she passed by with her uncle, Werner, the camp healer, giving Deiter an appraising look. "Ye best get used to it."

Dieter said nothing, but a frown formed upon his pale brow. Difficult to discern, Dieter and his thoughts always brought consternation to her. His mind, though complex, gave her comfort to know her brother thought deeply about his family and friends. As the other rebels gathered, he exchanged a nod with Bertolf then glanced beyond him looking about and then returned gaze to his recent peer in battle.

"Marttinen?" He quarried.

"Didn't make it," Bertolf said, smiling sadly. "Owed me, too."

As Dieter sighed again, Nerijus approached them, taking the center amidst the gathering rebels. "Right! So we be at the mouth o' the Widow's Trail, as Elias's callin' this place—here be where we planned t'meet der Flechtemann. Yet we can nay linger for long. I pray they reach us swiftly, lest a party of mercenaries latch upon our trail."

Anna glanced at the fading daylight, a tinge of worry in her anxious voice, she quarried Nerijus."Where will we be headin' now? Once they join us again?"

"Who knows," Nerijus muttered as he nervously surveyed the forest around them, his eyes scanning the trees as if seeking guidance for security. "There be a hidden valley to the east, but savior's teeth, I donna' want nay part of valleys nor mountains anymore. But the decision is upon der Flechtemann, when or if he returns."

Dieter shouldered his spear uncomfortably, catching an odd note in the comment. "Why says ye that? What does ye mean about Father? Why *if* he returns?"

Nerijus' gaze locked on the perceptive young man, uncertain how to respond. "I meant nothin' by it. I be just considerin' each possibility, lad."

Just then, those gathered heard the distant sound of galloping hooves. Anna, alert to the echo, caught her breath. The rebels tensed, listening to the distant roll as if a breath on the wind. Nerijus paused to hear, then exhaled.

"I detect naught but a dozen light riders," he said, relaxing. "It be our lads returnin'!"

"How could ye hear that?" Dieter incredulous, mumbled more audible than intended, glanced embarrassed to Nerijus then returned to the moment at hand and gripped his spear nervously.

Nerijus, already striding in the direction of the hoof-falls, when through the trees, hooded forms emerged atop the short, shaggy horses favored by the rebels.

"Well I'll be," Old Werner muttered nearby, with feigned incredulity. "I should take a look at yer ears one o' these days. They be far sharper than what be between them."

Nerijus made as if to retort, then paused, focusing on the approaching group. He became aware, something did not appear to be right. The recollection soon became apparent…the riders were one short.

The rebels, their cloaks billowing in the breeze, slowed as they approached. Nerijus, a knot forming in his stomach, stepped forward to greet them. As the figures dismounted, he scanned their faces, seeking the familiar visage of der Flechtemann. The formidable visage was nowhere to be found.

Sieghart, burdened with a weight heavier than any armor on his broad shoulders, took charge of the group. Elias came next, tears streaming down his pockmarked cheeks. His complexion was pale, and he appeared almost unwell, with vacant eyes fixed on the distance. Anna felt a lump in her throat as she observed her brother, Dieter. Sieg dismounted, and Dieter's grip on his spear intensified, sensing a grave discovery ahead.

His figure bore the full toll of his hardship. The flickering light of day amidst the forest shadow illuminated Yakov's features, revealing a face battered and bruised. Above his overgrown beard, his skin showed hellish yellow and purple where he bore the marks of his ordeal. A cruel scar, still recognizable, creased the side of his head where the hair still refused to regrow.

"Yakov," Anna said, her voice breaking, Her heart ached at the sight of her brother. As the siblings rushed forward, Dieter met Yakov's gaze, noticing the vacant look in his eyes.

210

Sieghart nodded weakly at Anna as she passed him, then spoke in a steady, but grieving voice. Standing in his saddle so all could hear he continued, "Nerijus—and ye rebels all, listen. We have brought our Yakov back, and the Chain is fallen—*but...*"

The word hung heavy in the air. Nerijus nodded slowly.

"Where's father?" Anna's voice broke the unsteady silence, as she and Dieter helped their brother down. Yakov turned away at the question. Sieghart looked down at her from his mount, heartache plain in his eyes. Not thinking, the word 'father' came easily to her without her usual venom. Yakov looked at her with tearful eyes.

Seeing his expression, she looked to Sieghart. Anna's eyes widened in realization, a sharp gasp escaping her lips. Dieter took a trembling breath, trying to avoid the conversation as he helped his brother limp forth. A single tear fell down Yakov's cheek.

"We lost 'im," Sieghart finally said, remorse beginning to crack the strength of his character. His words carried a weight that echoed without sound through the forest. His eyes glistening in the daylight as he continued, "Der Flechtemann saved Yakov by meetin' Petres the Chain on the field of combat where he slew the menace… But… from the wounds of battle...he nay survived."

The news hung in the air, a devastating revelation that shattered the fragile hope to which the rebels rallied, held by the mythical strength of der Flechtemann's cause. Anna's eyes suddenly welled with tears, and she collapsed to her knees sobbing uncontrollably. Hilda ran to her friend, embracing her in Anna's need for comfort. Dieter continued to silently help Yakov, as though unable to fully comprehend the news. Muttering began among the shocked partisans. Some of the men collapsed where they stood, sitting with their heads in their hands. Some arguing, desperate to poke holes in the assertion. Others, women and children, of the band sought to comfort or grieve in their own way.

"What? But ye didn't see anythin' aye…?"

"Nay, he's likely right behind ye…"

"Taken? Nay, nay, canna' be—"

"We saw it," Elias snapped, wiping a furious hand across his teary face.

Sieghart glanced at him, then continued, his voice heavy, commanding to be heard. "What we know now be Petres's men captured him, an'... though we saw our leader nay die, we can still fear the worst, fer the Abbot knows how dangerous der Flechtemann be, even he be gone. The Chain be dead—he hath taken our light with him, but nay the cause."

The forest felt as though it closed in around them. Yakov helped to sit, leaning on a tree near Dieter, his gaze fixed on the ground. Anna still sobbed nearby, as though years of suppressed emotion suddenly let loose. Red-eyed, she held Hilda and Dieter's hands, her brother silent, his eyes blank to his innermost thoughts.

The lines on his weathered face etched with sorrow, Nerijus went from sibling to sibling, patting their shoulders or hugging them. Tears hung low at the corners of his own eyes as he kneeled beside Yakov. Werner was poking and prodding at him already, forcing the wounded man to look up so he could observe the whites of his eyes.

"More yellowin' of the eye..." Werner muttered. "Ye has nay had enough water. Now ye run an' get me a waterskin, Neri."

Nerijus nodded, stood and left. Elias still sat motionless on his horse, his gaze turned to the darkening sky, as if expecting it to fall. Twilight now moved towards evening, and a furtive campfire was lit by Bertolf and one other.

As Yakov drank greedily, Sieghart still faced the increasingly unruly discontent that began to take its toll among the rebels. Their voices, full of confusion and grief, sounded out.

"May be that 'e lives," one of the rebels cried.

"If Yakov can be freed, why nay he!"

Sieghart, his eyes reflecting the same sorrow that gripped the camp, raised his hands in a gesture of command, a silent plea for order. "Quiet, all of ye! Shall ye dishonor his sacrifice with discord?"

The rebels remained in the grip of disgruntled uneasiness as Elias began to speak. Interested quiet revived the group momentarily as he took upon himself his position as one of the leaders in the band.

"Our Der Flechtemann suspected such might happen," the lanky rebel said in a bitter voice. "Fer he was wise. And he spoke t'us—Sieghart, Nerijus, and I—that if he be taken, know that he be lost. They would nay let him live, fer even the dirt at his boot is greater than they shall ever be in their silks, and now…" he paused attempting to stand with his acknowledged strength of will, "we need accept, he be…lost…"

Loosing to the emotion of the moment, Elias fell away into quiet sobs. The rebels paused to see the shattering of his usually stoic mien.

Sieghart, seeing the need to divert the attention of the others for Elias, continued conversations with a few vocal groups who would pay attention about unity and the cause. Most of the rebels, confused by the sudden news, mulled about aimlessly, not knowing what to do or say.

Amidst the chaos, Anna, continuing her lament, stood with Dieter's help. Together, the siblings made their way to Yakov. Quietly, Anna approached and wrapped her arms around him. Werner paused his examination, knowing enough to give them their space. The old man took his leave with gruff condolences. Dieter found a seat on a log nearby, shaking his head in unattached disbelief as he looked at Yakov.

For his part, Yakov's gaze lingered fixed on a distant point only he could see. The touch of his sister, though warm and comforting, felt far-off. Anna, still crying, whispered words of reassurance, trying to penetrate the dissociated fog that enveloped her brother.

"It nay naught yer fault, Yakov," Anna murmured, her voice barely audible above the sound of discussions around them. "Father made his choice, to save ye."

Yakov continued unresponsive refraining from any awareness his sister sat near. A fresh recollection of guilt and grief soon came to the surface of his face, the weight noticeably settled in the sag of his shoulders. Within him, a voice awakened… *Again, you have lived when the better man has died. Mikkel, Hans—and yet here you sit. Why?*

No answer came to assuage his feeling.

214

Sieghart, having managed to quell some of the dissent, approached the siblings. His tired expression softened, revealing the depth of his own mourning. "We'll be needin' to discuss next steps—but fer now, ye three need rest."

Dieter drawn now to Siegharts' voice listened, even as Anna and Yakov remained still. Around them, the rebels quieted slowly by ones and twos until Sieg could be heard.

As darkness enveloped the camp, the flickering campfires cast long shadows as the rebels, their faces etched with weariness and loss, sought solace in stories. They told tales of their der Flechtemann, remembering old escapades, enhancing what they remembered, giving life to a legend to be. What little alcohol remained among their sparse supplies was rationed around the fire as men and women sensed the end of an era. Sieghart and Elias sat together talking in low voices, even as Nerijus, alone, found solace as he fed the horses, too tired to think of the future.

The siblings remained huddled together.

Dieter thought about the father never given the chance to know, and a leader he often, in stubbornness, found at odds to follow.

Anna thought about the man who left their lives in a night long ago, only to return to interrupt their lifes' direction as a distant mask of what she remembered. Anna sobbed as she realized, under the veil, her father never left at all, but always protected the family.

Yakov didn't engage much with his surroundings, even though food and water brought some color back to him. He remained in a state of melancholic detachment from Anna, Dieter, and those who could be considered his family and friends. Seated near the campfire, his jutting cheekbones

215

caught the flickering light, while his long, dark hair obscured his eyes, blending with his beard. Weary eyes stared into the fire as Yakov Symon pondered various possibilities, while the transition from dusk of evening to the dark of night marked his weary contemplation.

Chapter XVII: Magdeburg

"And such is life's path—upon the close, we return to old paths, and much has changed. Suffering has stained us and the road—and we suffer to know that we are cursed to our old haunts...not knowing that God still lives in the places we left behind."

-Brother Jakob, circa 1382

Yakov, amazed at the sight before him became acutely aware of the pall of decay hanging heavy over the dark city like a shroud of death. Magdeburg reeled from the desolation of shadows in every corner, his years of absence only adding despair to the weary traveler.

Yakov moved through the square with a disoriented detachment, the air thick with a palpable sense of oppression. His dark hair hung to his shoulders as he looked around, remembering the last time he had come here. But the once-bustling marketplace frequented by the common folk was a shell of its former color, with many stalls abandoned entirely, and the cobblestones stained with neglect. Beggars lay drunk or dying on the peripheries of his vision, poisoned by the cheap, tainted alcohol the local merchants peddled. Beyond the guarded bridge to the city, summarily denied, those afflicted by sickness slept on the cloying earth or begged each day for entry into the confines of its security.

They would have lost all heart if they entered, however, for what waited within the city was scarce better than outside. Though opulence still adorned the spires of the rich, and wealth was still to be made along the Elbe, the access to its gleaming bosom was increasingly restricted. Regional merchant guilds, endorsed and supported by the Hansa, formed strangleholds over the imports and exports, and independent mercantile endeavors were increasingly doomed to failure. The economy reeled unevenly as the rich got richer, and those on the very precipice of attaining comfort fell back into destitution. Within Magdeburg proper, the corruption of the guards soared. Three buildings of enterprise burned down over the course of the past year for refusing to pay the city guard for protection. Semi-sanctioned by the hypocrisy of indulgence the Abbot received generous gifts from every crook of substance. Then turning to the crucifixion on the cross, embraced the appearance of piety in public for mass, praying for the suffering souls of Magdeburg.

As Yakov walked now through the narrow streets, Sieghart's somber gesture caught his attention. Elias's lanky frame was nearby as well, half-lost in the shadows.

The three of them entered the city earlier, one by one, disguised as merchants or wanderers looking for employment. Word received from others searching for their leader, der Flechtemann, placed him still alive here. Yakov the last to arrive among the searching rebels, read the truth already on Sieghart and Elias' pallid faces, but he willed himself forward, to greet them, each step almost too heavy to bear with the inevitable.

As Yakov approached, Sieghart and Elias met him in the desolate square. The air, tainted with the stench of human waste and the muck of decay, enveloped them, clogging their senses. Gorge momentarily rose in their throats as they paused in acknowledgement of the other. An errant fly landed on Yakov's cheek, but he failed to notice, as Sieg placed a comforting hand on his shoulder. When Sieg spoke, the words were ladened with burden and grief.

"We were…too late, Yakov. The execution—"

Yakov's heart sank, and the world around him blurred. Magdeburg melted into a surreal haze as he struggled to find his voice.

"So he is…gone? Truly so?"

"Aye," Sieghart nodded heavily.

"I... I needs t'be seein' him," Yakov uttered hesitantly, his words barely audible. Never loud, he grew quieter since his father's death, only audible to those who listened carefully.

Sieghart and Elias exchanged a glance. Sieg, with a solemn nod, gestured towards the darkened alleys leading to the place of der Flechtemann's, Yakov's father's, execution.

As he walked with Sieg and Elias, the air seemed to thicken, suffocating Yakov with the grim reality of the city's descent into darkness. What felt like years ago, Yakov and Mikkel, his dead friend, spent time in the Chain's command as mercenaries. It was here he realized the true nature of Petres the Chain and the Abbot. Here, too, Elias served as a scout for der Flechtemann, seeking to gather information and to deliver supplies taken by der Flechtemann, and the rebels, to help the citizenry of Megdeburg. Though at that time their paths did not cross, they would in time. The past felt lost in the death of the man Yakov now was able to call father, Hans Symon, der Flechtemann. The light of will now shown dimly in the city having leached away by the strife caused by subversion of the masses. Though children still played in the alleys, their gaze was hostile and cautious. Yakov could only shudder at each encounter.

The execution square, now desolate, long devoid of participants, displayed only its inverted cross hanging from an iron chain in a distant corner. Sieghart pointed in the direction of the grotesque apparatus of death. Yakov, overcome for a moment with emotion, could only question the obscene purpose of such a spectacle? Bloody nails still hammered inside, with blood now black and congealed, pooling below the upside-down symbol of sacrilege.

"They named him antichrist," Elias breathed, his face twisted with aggrieved malevolence. "And so they slew a saint."

"… hung, drawn, and quartered," Sieghart muttered, his voice gravelly with grief.

The revelation hit Yakov like a physical blow. Horror and nausea churned within him as he beheld the gruesome aftermath of his father's demise. The church, complicit in the desecration, had sanctioned the atrocity, and the square bore witness to the twisted brutality of those who hid behind the habit. The notion became obvious to Yakov, the execution was for the witness and not for the accused; for he knew, dead was dead. The only thing the gruesomeness of the occasion could stir in the hearts of the kin of the deceased was further anger and hatred toward the perpetrator at the insult of the mutilation. Mothers and fathers have sons and daughters, and all are aggrieved at the sight of the mistreatment of the remains of the loved and cherished. Yakov held close, no difference in feeling anger

220

or remorse could be found in any generation. Now anger rose in their hearts…not the anger resulting in retribution, but the anger which led to change.

Yakov, overcome with anguish, felt bile rise in his throat again. Sieghart grieved in silence, his gaze fixed on the ground, while Elias, pallid and sickened, still stared at the cross as if willing it for a sign.

Unknown to Yakov or Sieghart, Elias managed a final act of defiance in der Flechtemann's name. He bribed the guards to secure a small measure of redemption for der Flechtemann's remains, ensuring at least most of him, found sanctuary on holy ground.

In another solemn gesture, Elias drew from his belt Der Flechtemann's rondel dagger, secured with yet another bribe. Pushing it at Yakov's chest, he spoke in an iron voice, eyes fixed with intent on Yakov's, "To ye falls thy father's burden."

The cold metal, still stained with the Chain's blood, felt alien in Yakov's trembling hands. He remembered this dagger at his own throat. Now he could feel the dagger of Petres' death sinking into the adversary. The feeling brought him no joy or release from his sorrow, but part of his father was now returned to him—and with it, something else visited upon him.

Noticing Yakov's gaze beyond the knife, Sieghart spoke. "Elias an' I be talkin', Yakov. Truth be yer father sacrificed himself fer the rebellion. He believed in something greater than any one of us—an' now, it falls upon ye to carry tha' legacy."

Elias nodded. "Ye be his heir, and thus should ye be the face of der Flechtemann, embodiment o' our rebellion.

Our folk need someone to rally behind, someone t'carry on his torch. Tha' barer needs be ye."

Yakov, still grappling with the horrors of his father's demise, felt the weight of their words only dimly. "He didn't die fer the rebellion. He sacrificed himself fer me—fer his children. His family." He argued.

Elias looked at him dispassionately, while Sieg nodded and placed his hands on Yakov's shoulders. He looked at Yakov with clear, focused eyes. "Ye may be right at that," Sieghart said, his eyes still locked onto Yakov. "Yer father knew the risks, and aye, he chose to sacrifice himself fer ye, fer Anna, fer Dieter. But though he died fer ye, he lived fer *his cause*—the very cause ye suffered for."

Yakov nodded, not knowing what to say.

"Now," Sieghart continued, shaking Yakov slightly. "Ye must become the symbol o' this rebellion. The legend of der Flechtemann must survive."

"Aye," Elias finally said, his gaze steady. "But worry nought—we shall nay burden thee, Yakov. Ye shall have our support, whilst we stand behind thee, guiding thy arm and directin' yer command. We know the burden o' the cause be too great fer any one man but der Flechtemann to carry alone—and so we shall bear it wi' ye."

So, they shall run the show, whispered the constant voice within him. *But you, Yakov, you will be the face that is praised and hated!*

Though he and his father spoke about this very line of transfer, he was not sure he could carry it off. He was not sure he would have the backing of the band at large. The twisted logic of the proposal did not seem much amiss, however. To his thinking pressing forward the cause would

222

be the only logical stamp of acceptance upon the harsh reality that awaited the rebels. Only this small triad knew his father was gone, so accepting the leadership in his name may work. For sure the 'cause' must not die. Too much good depended on the survival of the legend and the goals intended.

Yakov, his voice barely rising above a whisper, finally spoke with some reluctance, "Fine. I'll take on the mantle of thy cause."

The walls, indifferent to the clandestine pact formed amidst them, bore witness to the birth of a reluctant leader. Yakov, now a shadow of der Flechtemann, embraced the weight of the rebellion.

Sieghart clapped his back. Elias, however, always the forward thinker now thought about possibilities ahead of the rebel band.

"To stay here now be both futile an' foolhardy," Elias muttered. "We must leave, one at a time, o'course, and I shall be leavin' at dark. Sieg, ye shall ride out with party o' yeoman on the morrow as well—and Yakov, ye shall leave with the wagon ye arrived beside. We have paid 'im well fer his secrecy. And, I remind ye, visit nay yer father's grave, fer it may be watched. Instead we shall hold a funeral back at camp where we can make general the knowledge of der Flechtemann's transfer. Our leader and yer father, Hans Symon, hath passed, but der Flechtemann will live on."

They nodded to each other, and as they dispersed into the desolate evening, a sense of purpose enveloped each of them. The rebellion, though fractured and twisted, would endure—and thus, the struggle would continue.

***

The days passed, and the darkness of this place where Yakov now found himself staying, weighed on him. It creaked under his feet. It ate at the edge of his mind, and nauseated, Yakov could no longer stay in the dingy, unkempt room given him. Walking furtively out into the city was scarcely better. Yakov felt faint, until he saw the satiny, burnished face of what hinted to him the structure of an old church. The ancient building's arched brow called to him, and his footfalls answered.

The cold stone of the holy place embraced Yakov as he wandered into its confines, seeking solace in the dimly lit sanctuary. The oppressive stench of the city seemed to momentarily dissipate within the sacred walls. Here the smell of linen, old wood, and faint rosewater gratefully encouraged his senses with each breath he drew.

Yakov found a corner, the shadows converging around him. As he sat in quiet contemplation, the flickering candles cast dancing shadows on the walls. With a sigh that carried the weight of his countless sorrows, Yakov raised his eyes to the dimly lit altar.

"O Father…who art in heaven," Yakov whispered, his voice a murmur in the sacred hush. "I have not prayed to thee since I was…young. Very young. Mine mother asked it o' me, so blame her nought. I only came upon thee the long way around. If ye be listenin', I come to beseech ye."

The silence seemed expectant, Yakov continued. "Accept my father into yer heaven. Let him wander under yon green boughs. He deserves such, fer though his death be in our name, his life was sacrificed to yer flock." The candles glowed dully in the dark, and Yakov's quiet plea was hushed by the silence. But he continued, his words carrying a raw sincerity. "And Lord my God, if ye know mercy, grant him the peace in death that eluded him in life."

Moments passed, and Yakov's distant gaze remained fixed on the altar, his eyes wet as he continued. "In truth," Yakov admitted in a hollow voice, "all I ever wanted was a peaceful life. A life far removed from the turmoil o' war an' responsibility. I wished to play among yer trees. I wished to drink from yer streams. I was born with heaven in me heart, and I sought it true—yet here, I found only manifold hells. But I s'pose peace be never meant fer us as suffer on this earth."

He smiled sadly.

As Yakov sat in contemplative silence, a priest in muted vestments approached, his footsteps muffled by the quiet reverence of the church. The aging cleric, with a stained white beard and gentle curiosity in his eyes, spoke softly, "Have ye lost someone, my son?"

Yakov nodded in acknowledgment. "Aye," he replied softly.

The priest, sensing the gravity of Yakov's sorrow, crossed himself and pressed further. "May I ask who ye hath lost, my son? Perhaps I can offer ye some comfort in yer hardship, fer company is sweet in sorrow."

"I have lost but a great man," Yakov answered, his gaze shifting from the priest to the altar beyond, moist eyes flickering in the candlelight.

The priest waited for more, but none seemed forthcoming. Yet the old man respected the quiet dignity in Yakov's grief. With a solemn nod, he left Yakov to his thoughts, disappearing into the shadows. The blazing

225

candles continued their dance as Yakov, with a heavy heart, rose from his corner.

Exiting the warm safety of the church, Yakov reentered the chilly reality outside—a world teeming with the anticipation of conflict, the flames of war, the challenges of struggle, and the pursuit of retribution, where all the myriad troubles that come with being human coexisted in perfect accord. However, as the weighty doors groaned closed behind him, Yakov faced the future without fear. Whatever was destined to unfold would do so. He was ready to play his role, and in due course, whether for better or worse, his day, too, would end.

Chapter XVIII: Epilogue

"And in the end all things end—and in ending, begin anew..."

-Brother Jakob, circa 1384

Michael sat with steepled hands as James read out the final word on the page. They were back at the Guten Tisch, Michael's coffee now gone cold, where they finished pouring over their transcription of this section of the old tome.

Outside the quaint diner, a quiet drizzle continued, darkening the asphalt as rain pattered over the tiled roofs. People entered the establishment to get out of the cold, shrugging in yellow parkas and steel-grey jackets. The warmth, a welcome respite from the weather outside, which tried to seep into the very floor—here was a place of human gathering always active, always in the moment.

Yet between Michael and James, the words from the journal seemed to linger in the air, a story which waited across centuries to connect them to the distant past. Today, the active diner, in which the two sat, drifted long forgotten in their awareness as they toiled over this portion of the folio to achieve their goal of completing the final parts of this section. So far, digested between the two researchers, the worn pages revealed a tale of rebellion, suffering, and sacrifice far more involved than anything Michael could have conceivably imagined when he came hunting for signs around the revelations of kin. Coming here, he expected to connect dots over old traces and clues, for sure, but trying to piece together a narrative of family and culture from

227

seemingly nothing appeared tedious at best. Instead, though, he found a fascinating tale lying in wait over the centuries, as though purely for his benefit. Now, he reveled in the old monk's tale, shaking his head as he tried to absorb the enormity of what James and he recovered from the transcription on this rainy afternoon.

"So Der Flechtemann died," Michael said eventually, then answering his own question. "Right, I shouldn't be surprised. I half expected a daring raid and rescue, but history tends not to be so dramatic."

James raised an eyebrow, pointing at the book. "What, all this isn't dramatic enough for you?"

"Puzzling, more like," Michael shook his head again.

"True. Yakov walked out of one church and, many years later, walked right into another," James mused, his eyes scanning the transcribed words. "How did things get to that? Nothing seems quite *that* godly about this lad. I've known atheists who have gone to church more often than him—so what could possibly convince him to cloister himself later in life ?"

"Runaway perhaps," Michael thought aloud, his gaze fixed on the pages before him. He remembered the tears, then. "Or perhaps just for some peace—Lord knows this man saw far too much. His suffering was terrible."

"Did he? 'See far too much', that is. Don't we all have moments in our lives we 'see far too much, sometimes. And yet he still made it," James shook his head. "Don't know how he'd fare as his old man's heir, but he certainly showed his tenaciousness."

Michael nodded absently as he pondered the enigma of Yakov's journey. *Here was the tale of a man who joined—*

228

and perhaps led—a rebellion against a feudal system, the church, and nobility of all stripes, yet somehow emerged on the other side, presumably living out the end of his days in the sacred walls of a monastery.

"Earth to Michael," James said with a worried smile at Michael's distant glare. "You seem less than happy—it's not like you to be impatient. If that's anyone, it's me."

Michael chuckled. "I suppose I'm a bit invested."

"Fair enough. I mean, sure, we're a bit confounded so far, but maybe we finally have some answers," James suggested, glancing at his older companion. "For one thing, we can tell how he learned to read and write—Elias taught Yakov some Latin letters for that code of theirs, so it's pretty likely he taught him more, like reading and writing in Latin, maybe even this old local script he peppers in."

Michael sighed, before smiling wryly. "Conjecture, my dear Watson. Can't be certain—could be he learned more elsewhere. And what about Sieghart, Anna, and Dieter? What about this Elias fellow?" Michael asked, his eyes glancing at the pages for answers that remained elusive. "What could have happened to them…? Yakov, for better or worse, seems committed to this cause, and certainly to his family. He wouldn't leave them, would he?"

"Or," James interjected delicately. "Maybe they didn't all make it through. Those were tough enough days, and if I have my timeline right, things would only get worse after this. Plague, wars, increased corruption and levies, mass migrations, socio-economic upheaval—it was all happening."

"Sounds very 21st century, doesn't it," Michael muttered. "These questions are hard on the old heart, I tell you. I'll be up all night once more thinking about the similarities."

James, taking on role of the voice of reason for a change, gently reminded him, "Come on, Michael. You know we'll discover the truth in due time—the journal has led us this far, hasn't it? I believe patience can be our guide."

"What if it's incomplete?" Michael said worriedly, then caught James' frank look and chuckled. "Right, you're right. We'll get there when we get there."

"Right."

"And it's not the end of the world even if it's incomplete, right? I came here expecting nothing, so this is more than enough for me." Michael agreed.

"Good!"

"…Even if I'll never sleep again unless I know how all this ends?"

James rolled his eyes. "There's such a thing as obsession, y'know. And look. Besides…" He said, laughing and picking up Michael's mug, "… your coffee's gone to ice. I'll get you another, wait—"

As the younger man rose to order another round of coffee, the spell that wrapped them in a reverie of thought and idea during their research broke. With sudden awareness, Michael could hear the other patrons and smell the freshly baked desserts the diner was selling. Around him, the people were muted but alive. They were less noisy than the crowd he was familiar with, but on their faces were the familiar human emotions, unchanged for thousands of years—love, happiness, sorrow, boredom, and so much more. They were as fascinating to study and observe as the

230

book he and James set aside for a moment. And, as Michael leaned back in his chair, he caught a glimpse of his own face in the glass window beside him.

Just for that fleeting moment, Michael fancied he could see an old, tired monk looking back at him.